BEGIN RUMBLE STRIP

By R. Scott Bolton

Copyright 2022 by R. Scott Bolton
ISBN: 978-0-9997962-4-5

A Rough Edge Studios Production
www.roughedgestudios.com

Other books by R. Scott Bolton

From the Adventures of H. B. Fist
KILLED BY DEATH
OVERNIGHT SENSATION
BURNER

Brace Heller Novels
KNIFEPOINT

Standalones
DEAD DICK

For Shelley.
Who Loves Hawaii. Especially Kauai.

As always, thanks to my ever-vigilant Quality Control Team. The readers listed below offered opinions and corrections that helped form the completed work, and I can never thank them enough for their input. But I'll try: Thanks to Shelley Bolton, Josh Bolton, Doug Bolton, Sue Bolton, John DeRuvo, Denise & Joe Lopiano, Steve Snider, and Jeff Rogers.

Also, a special shout-out to the National Novel Writing Month non-profit organization. Each November, they challenge their participants to write a novel in thirty days. I started in 2013 and have completed the first draft of a novel every year since. BEGIN RUMBLE STRIP was one of those. I heartily recommend NaNoWriMo to anyone who is considering writing a novel, screenplay, stage play or whatever. NaNoWriMo helps keep you focused. Check them out and feel free to donate: www.nanowrimo.org.

CHAPTER ONE

Lynn Fuller was one of those people you knew you didn't like from the very first time you met her. She was cold, she was sanctimonious, and she had a personality like the mouth feel of a persimmon. Her face clung to her skull like a taut rubber mask and her range of emotions was limited to perhaps three.

Today, however—four weeks after I had first met Ms. Fuller—I was actually looking forward to talking with her.

Fuller was the Human Resources director of a health tech company based in Santa Maria called DiabetiCorp. It was a Fortune 500 company that manufactured and sold medical equipment for diabetics. Glucose meters, test strips, lancets, and such. Just over a month ago, Diabeti-

Corp, through Fuller, had hired me to shadow one of their employees, a Miss Nina Spencer, to keep track of her time from the moment she arrived in the morning until the time she left for home in the evening. They wanted me to make note of when she clocked out for lunch and when she clocked back in for work. They did not ask me to follow her to or from work, or to or from lunch. They just wanted me to keep track of the actual time she spent at work. Morning in. Evening out. Lunch in. Lunch out. Keep a diary. Report back to Fuller after thirty days and they would pay me enough money to cover my mortgage for three months.

It was one of those jobs that was easy to say yes to. It was like taking candy from a baby. And now, thirty days later, I was ready to get paid.

And have a little fun doing it.

I sat in a repugnant leather and chrome chair in the hallway outside the Human Resources office, listening to the receptionist repeat, "DiabetiCorp, how may I direct your call?" over and over again, the monotonous drone of her voice never wavering a single note. I was impressed with her dedication. I don't know how you could say the same phrase 800 times a day without changing it up just a little bit, but she was a master.

The dog-eared copy of Men's Health magazine that stared up at me from the table near my knees did nothing to draw my attention, despite the HOW MATTHEW McCONAUGHEY STAYS FIT AND RUGGED headline plastered across a close-up photo of the actor's decidedly craggy face.

A thin tinkle of what sounded like circus music trickled out of a hidden speaker somewhere, at a volume that made you wonder if you were actually hearing music or if someone was watching TV on the floor above you.

It was cool in the office, which I appreciated. I'll take air conditioning over tepid staleness any day of the week.

I glanced at my Apple Watch, ostensibly to check for text or e-mail messages but really to note the time. It was just about 4:15pm. I had been waiting for almost forty-five minutes. Fuller had asked me to meet her today at 3:30pm and the excitement was wearing off. *Give her another ten minutes*, said a little voice in my head, *and then we're out of here.* Thankfully, another, more logical voice in my head spoke up: *Um, we're not going anywhere. We got to get paid, remember?*

Fortunately, I didn't have to wait another ten minutes to find out which voice would win. The phone on the receptionist's desk gave a funny little chirp and she reached up and touched a hidden button on her microphone, muting her next barrage of "DiabetiCorp, how may I direct your call?"

"She'll see you now," she said with a plastic smile. "Go right in."

"Thank …" I started. But she was already back to it.

"DiabetiCorp, how may I direct your call?"

I stood, somehow managing to break eye contact with the stunning Mr. McConaughey's baby blues, and stepped toward the only door in the hallway. It was painted eggshell white, exactly like the walls around it and, except for the fact there was a bronze knob sticking out of it, you would never have guessed there was a door there. I turned the knob, pulled and, with a weird sucking sound, the door peeled open.

The office inside was ridiculously cavernous and far-cically Spartan. The walls inside were painted a powder blue, the thick carpet that covered the floor a slightly darker shade of the same. A large, dark brown desk that was probably made from one of the last great redwoods sat facing away from the room's floor-to-ceiling window, with its view of sprawling housing tracts fading out to towering mountains in the distance. The enormous desk looked tiny in the otherwise vacant room. *Why do people with corner offices always sit with their backs to the window?* I wondered, and then realized it was probably some kind of power thing.

Lynn Fuller sat behind the desk, staring up at me ex-pectantly with eyes that were as cool as a viper's but spar-kled with a hint of excitement. She wore a black business pantsuit that looked expensive and professional but that could be best described as severe. She didn't stand or say a word but simply used her heavily-ringed fingers to indi-cate one of the two transparent polycarbonate chairs in front of her desk. I sat in the one on the opposite end of the single Tiffany lamp on the left side of her desk. Its richly designed metal base and stained-glass shade seemed wildly out of place in the ultra-modern office space.

There were only two other things on Fuller's desk: A blue-lined, yellow-paged notepad and what looked like a very expensive pen resting beside it. They seemed exactly parallel to each other, as though the distance between them had been measured carefully.

I wondered where her phone was and realized she probably kept it tucked away inside a desk drawer.

"Mr. Heller," Fuller said with a phony fluorescent brightness. The artificial emotion behind it reminded me of the robots from *Westworld*. "The Shorts and Sandals Detective."

I wasn't wearing shorts or sandals and I hated that goddamn article the L.A. Times had written about me. And now they were talking *movie!*

"That's not something I'm proud of," I said.

"I can imagine," Fuller said. "It wasn't very flattering."

"You'll get no argument from me."

She offered me a sterile smile. "Thank you for meeting with me."

I nodded. "You said 3:30."

"Oh?" Fuller said, her eyes widening in saccharin surprise. "What time is it?"

"4:20," I said. "You should probably get a clock in here."

"Clocks are for peasants," Fuller said. "Besides, I was under the impression I was paying for your time."

"That ended at midnight last night," I said. "I'm on my own time. Our agreement was for thirty days."

She gave me a look that said I was being unreasonable. "I'm sorry you had to wait," she said with no sorrow whatsoever. "I've been very busy."

"I'm sure you have."

"So," she said, delighted that I'd moved on. "I take it you have a report for me?"

"I do." I slid the manila folder I'd been carrying onto the smooth-as-glass top of her desk. It drifted over to her side as though on a cushion of air. I wondered how many times a day that desk was polished.

And not by Fuller.

She caught the folder with her fingertips and spun it around so that the open side was on her right. She peeled back the front cover and used her other hand to remove the short stack of printed paper within. Her eyes scanned the first page, then the second page, and so on. Her frozen face never changed until she came to the last page. I saw her eyebrow give a tiny jump and then she looked up at me.

"Your invoice?" she asked, holding it up and giving it a little wave.

"As agreed."

"That's a lot of money."

"As agreed," I repeated.

"A rather easy assignment, wasn't it?" Fuller asked.

"Easy, yes," I said. "But I've spent the past four weeks of my life up here. You're paying me for my time, as much as for my expertise."

Fuller waved at the air. "No, no," she said. "You misunderstand. We will pay you every dollar we promised. What I'm saying is that it was an easy assignment and you're probably wondering why in the world we hired you."

I gave her a grim smile. At this point, there were two ways this conversation could go. I decided to let it play out just a little longer.

"Not my place to wonder," I said. "You didn't pay me to be a consultant. You paid me to keep track of an employee."

"Yes, but didn't you wonder why? Weren't you even a little bit curious as to what we were looking for?"

I thought a moment, and then nodded. "All right," I said. "Sure, I was. Especially when, after a month, it looks to me like Miss Spencer is pretty much the model employee. She arrives to work on time, she leaves work on time. She barely has any overtime at all. Her lunch breaks are thirty to thirty-five minutes long. She takes them in the park near the first floor. As far as I can tell, she's not abusing company time, she's not stealing company secrets and she's not bothering any of her colleagues about anything." I nodded again. "So, yes, I'm a little curious as to why you wanted to spend all this money for someone to watch her when, as far as I can tell, she's not doing anything wrong."

Fuller's smile was ghoulish as she tucked my report into the manila folder and closed it. She folded her hands, interlocking her fingers, and leaned forward across the desk. "Oh, but she is, Mr. Heller, she is. And this report proves it." Her eyebrows climbed her forehead and I could sense she was waiting for me to bite. I wasn't in the biting mood.

"She's committing fraud," Fuller said after a moment, her smile fading into a flat line of disappointment and anger. "She's lying on her timecard."

I scrunched up my eyes. "How is that possible?" I asked. "She worked a little less than ninety minutes overtime the entire month. She got to the office on time and she headed for home on time, every night virtually the same. She didn't even take her morning breaks most days. I don't see any room for her to lie about how much she worked."

Fuller smiled again. "Oh, she isn't lying about how *much* she worked," she told me, tapping the folder with her fingertips. "She's lying about *when* she works."

Fuller opened the folder, flipped through a couple of pages, and then pointed.

"Here," she said. "Ms. Spencer clocked in at 8:00am and clocked out at 5:01pm. She took her lunch from 12:00pm to 12:30pm."

"Sounds like the perfect day," I said.

"But it's not," Fuller said. "Because she actually took her lunch from 12:45pm to 1:15pm."

"What difference does that make?" I asked. "A half hour is a half hour."

"Because she's committing a crime, Mr. Heller," Fuller said, closing the folder dramatically. "She's falsifying her timecard." She flicked the folder away. It floated halfway across the desk on its invisible cushion and then spun to a stop. Fuller sat back in her chair, her reptilian eyes daring me to question her.

"She worked the exact number of hours she reported every day," I said. "To the minute. She likes to take a late lunch and the company won't let her."

"We have designated meal periods, Mr. Heller."

"*Rigid* meal periods," I said. "Ironclad and immobile."

"That is correct."

"But what harm did she do by taking a late lunch? You still got the hours you paid for out of her."

"*It's state law!*" Fuller spat vehemently, sitting suddenly forward like a cobra. "Really, Mr. Heller, I don't see your point here. She broke the law, she violated company policy and now she will be terminated."

I leaned back in my transparent chair. It creaked and settled back a little farther than I liked. For a moment, I thought I was going to go right over backward. "How's her work?" I asked, after the chair settled safely. "Is she a good employee?"

"I don't see how that's any business of yours," Fuller said.

"Humor me."

There was a 50/50 chance she'd tell me just to get the hell out of her office, but I was betting she was too head-strong to just throw me out without putting me in my place. "Ms. Spencer has been an excellent employee," she said after a moment, but I could see her distaste as she said it. "She has a spotless record, has showed significant improvement in the two years she's worked here, and her personnel folder is filled with nothing but high praise from her co-workers and superiors." Her eyes sparkled with crocodile tears. "Unfortunately, we cannot tolerate fraud. She will be missed."

"If it weren't for the mis-reported lunch times," I said. "What other reason would you have to let her go?"

"That's more than enough, Mr. Heller," Fuller said. "She broke the law. She's done."

"So, if it weren't for the so-called fraud," I said. "You wouldn't be able to fire her, am I right?"

"That's correct. Although California is an 'At Will' state, Ms. Spencer has a contract with the company. There are certain guidelines that come into play."

"Speaking of that, why didn't you call her in? Write her up?"

"There was no need to. Timecard fraud is an instantly fireable offense."

I nodded. "So DiabetiCorp spent $3,000 to hire a private detective to monitor an exemplary employee's time just so they could fire her?"

"It seemed the best way to prevent any possible accusation against the company," Fuller said. "An outside third party has no dog in the hunt, as they say. We wanted to keep this on the up and up."

"I see," I said. "So, this has nothing to do with the fact that Miss Spencer and your husband have been having an affair for the past six months."

Fuller froze instantly. It was as though someone had punched her in the throat. Her mouth worked silently for a moment and then she croaked out, "How did you know that?"

"I'm a detective," I said. "It's what I do. You didn't really think I was going to come in here and just take a stopwatch to someone, did you? I knew from the moment you hired me that there was more here than meets the eye. And it didn't take much for me to uncover the big picture. There's not a lot to do in this town but eat steak and drink wine, so I spent my evenings tailing the woman you paid me to keep an eye on. Little did I know it would take me to the Skyview Motel and my client's husband."

"I want you out of here," Fuller said, her voice coming back demonstrably. "I want you the hell out of my office, now!"

I stood. "There's always more to the story," I said. "It's what I love about my job."

Fuller pounded on the table. "GET OUT!"

I nodded and moved toward the door, stopped halfway there, and turned back toward her.

"Just one more thing," I said, doing my best Columbo impersonation. "That'll be three grand, please."

Chapter Two

It's about a two-hour drive from Santa Maria to Ventura and I was glad to be making it for the last time, at least for a while. It wasn't a bad drive with the ocean on your right and the hilly scenery on the left, but it was lonely and, with only a stack of Cheap Trick, Motorhead and Black Sabbath CDs to keep me company, it always seemed to take me longer than two hours to get home.

For the DiabetiCorp gig, I'd driven up on Sunday evenings and stayed at a sleazy hotel paid for by the company during the week. Then back home Friday night to be with Marina and Wurzel and then back to work Sunday evening. It was something I'd rather not have done but 3K was 3K. I was glad to be heading home to stay for a while. Kick back at the office, return some calls and maybe take a few pictures of straying husbands in my own hometown for once.

I stayed South on the 101, passing through Buellton and signs promising SPLIT PEA SOUP and EVERYTHING FOR THE TRAVELER. I passed Isla Vista and reminisced about the Ramones show I was supposed to see there one night decades ago but wound up missing because my buddy got drunk and passed out in my car. I came to the traffic squeeze in Santa Barbara and slowed to a crawl, wondering which new beers they'd served up at The Brewhouse that was just off the next exit. The traffic cleared and I sailed past Carpinteria, promising myself to take Marina back there to grab a couple of beers at Island Brewing Company and then dinner at The Palms. Then I was in the final stretch, as the day darkened to night, cruising along with the Pacific Ocean sparkling on my right and catching sight of the city glow of Ventura as I came around the last bend.

I drove straight to my house and felt a jolt of excitement as I saw Marina's Mazda in the driveway. I parked beside it, climbed out of the car and—leaving my luggage in the car for now—jogged to the front door and entered the house.

Inside, the lights were dim and the temperature warm but bearable. The scent of hot tortilla soup flowed gently through the air, and I could feel the four weeks of Santa Maria time-keeping lift off my shoulders, making me feel lighter and calm.

"Honey! I'm home!" I called.

But it wasn't Marina who came sprinting around the kitchen, arms outstretched for her loving partner. Instead, it was Wurzel, his long doggy legs scrambling to get a purchase on the kitchen tile as he barreled toward me, tongue lolling, whining happily that daddy was here. He hit me at just above the knee, leapt up to kiss my face and the next thing I knew I was on the ground beside him, tousling his ears, rubbing his belly, and not managing to avoid a single doggy kiss.

A moment later, I noticed Marina standing above us, looking down with a smile that was halfway between disgusted disbelief and adoring love. She sipped at the glass of red wine in her hand and shook her head sadly.

"That dog gets a better welcome than I do," she said.

"Did you make tortilla soup?" I asked.

"Yes."

"Then you get a better welcome than the dog."

"I should hope so."

I pushed Wurzel away, stood, and pulled Marina into my arms.

"You home for a while now?" she asked.

"Back at the office tomorrow," I said. "I'm almost afraid to see the pile of mail there."

"You don't get any mail there," Marina said.

I looked hurt. "I get McDonald's coupons and solar power flyers."

"What you need to get," Marina said. "Are more checks."

"I got *this* one," I said, reaching into my back pocket and pulling out an envelope with "DiabetiCorp" printed in the return address area.

Marina tore it open, and her eyes widened. "Three thousand dollars," she said. "Not bad for a month's work."

"Almost paid for the gas."

"Yeah. Almost." She took another sip of her wine. "You ready to eat?"

"I'm ready," I said. "Managed not to stop at the Brewhouse and get their Hot Dog and a Beer special."

"What will power!"

We moved into the kitchen where I quickly poured a huge bowl of kibble for Wurzel ("That's too much for him!" cried Marina) while she spooned out a couple of bowls of her homemade tortilla soup. We sat and ate quietly, talking softly about our weeks, enjoying the simple meal and the fact that we were together. Wurzel noisily finished his kibble and curled up beneath the table, pretending to sleep but secretly hoping that some morsel of food might fall his way (as it did when I dropped a crinkle cut carrot slice near his nose). Marina gave me a disapproving look but took the sting out of it with a sweet smile.

We finished our meal, did the dishes, and retired to the couch where watched repeats of *30 Rock* and *Fresh off the Boat* via the miracle of streaming.

Sit-coms, the greatest American art form.

When we were finally laugh-tracked out, it was off to bed, both of us too tired and too content for anything but a good night's sleep.

The last thing I thought before I drifted off to sleep was that it was good to be home and good to know there was no place else I had to be for a long, long time.

CHAPTER THREE

"Brace, I need you to come to Kauai. I need your help."

That was the only message on the beat-up Panasonic answering machine that sat beside the ancient rotary dial phone on my equally ancient desk. My office was in the same building that Erle Stanley Gardner had created Perry Mason in, back in the 1930s, so I guess you could call my office ancient, too.

I had come in this morning feeling like a new man. It felt so good to be back at work, to once again be wearing the shorts and sandals that the Los Angeles Times (and soon, so they said, Paramount Pictures) had made infamous. What fresh mysteries would the future hold for me? What nefarious incidents had occurred in Ventura during my time away that required my attention? How many McDonald's coupons and solar power company flyers had arrived in my mail slot?

The answers were less than exciting. There was one message on the machine from someone wanting me to go to Kauai, there were no calls or texts from Lt. Steven Powell of the Ventura Police Department regarding nefarious events and there were no McDonald's coupons. All I got was a sheet of worthless BOGO coupons from Carl's Jr and a flyer from an aluminum siding company informing me IT'S A NEW DIMENSION IN MODERN LIVING!

I cracked the window behind the desk and stood there a moment, inhaling the familiar air. As usual, it was a perfect blend of automobile exhaust and fresh sea salt. It was early, still rush hour, so that exhaust scent would fade in an hour or so and the sea salt would take over. I walked back to my desk and fell into the leather chair behind my desk, sighing deeply.

There was one last possibility. I powered up the computer, opened my browser, and checked my e-mail. Nope. Nothing there either.

Looks like I was stuck with the guy in Kauai. If he was calling about a time share, I was going to hunt him down and shoot him in the neck.

I punched the PLAY button on the answering machine and listened to the message again. As I listened, I sat forward, realizing I should have paid more attention the first time through.

"Brace, it's Tracy Vang. Long time no see, brother. Hope you're doing well. Listen, Malu's in some serious trouble, got himself mixed up in some truly serious shit. Brace, I need you to come to Kauai. I need your help. Please give me a call as soon as you get this. Thanks."

I sat back, tilting back my chair, and putting my Teva'd feet up on the desk. Tracy Vang. I hadn't heard from him directly in nearly twenty years although we kept track of each other via Facebook like most old friends do these days. He was an old high school buddy of mine, a surfer and a poet, one of the nicest people I'd ever met.

Tracy always managed to remain cool and calm, no matter what the situation. His infectious, congenial smile, which seemed to be permanently affixed to his face, managed to make you feel that everything was going to be all right, no matter the odds. I'd admired him not only for his cool attitude but his amazing business savvy and work ethic. He'd gone from stoned surfer high school student to creating his own empire in about five years. Vang Surf LLC was a massive company that Tracy had built from scratch. Today, it was still one of the largest manufacturers of surf boards and surf attire in the world, and Tracy had become a bit of a celebrity himself. Like Richard Branson and his Virgin Group, Tracy was known the world round due to his adventurous ways and delightful demeanor, a fact that his marketing team played up to the fullest.

But now Tracy's son, Malu, was in trouble and he needed my help. Strange that I hadn't seen anything on the news. When the son of someone with as big a public profile as Tracy Vang gets into trouble, it was usually all over TV and the internet in a heartbeat.

I glanced at the time punch on the answering machine. Tracy had called the night before, at about 8pm. That would be 5pm his time. It was 8:30am now, which meant 5:30am his time. Too early to call. I leaned forward, opened the browser, and did some Google searching. Lots about Tracy and his skydiving trips to South America, and his delivery of Vang brand shoes to barefooted kids in Bangladesh, but nothing about his son Malu being in trouble.

And what kind of trouble? Tracy had said "some truly serious shit," but parents often exaggerated. Maybe Malu had got in with a bad crowd and was selling pot or something. Maybe he'd joined a street gang. (Were there street gangs in Kauai? I did another quick Google search. There were.) Maybe he'd been kidnapped. Hell, maybe he'd just got someone pregnant. At this point, I didn't know, and I wouldn't know until I got the chance to speak with Tracy.

I dicked around in the office a little bit. Shuffled some files, reviewed my accounting, read some newspapers. I went over to the window to confirm that the exhaust smell had diminished and indeed it had. The salty smell of the ocean was much stronger than it had been half an hour ago.

I sat back at the desk, thought about going to get some donuts, decided against it. I pulled up TMZ to see if there was any breaking news about Malu Vang and was unsurprised to find there was not. I found myself in a YouTube loop, clicking from one video to the next following Tracy's never-ending worldwide tour. His infectious smile and those damn ridiculous sunglasses he designed and sold made me grin and shake my head. Vang sunglasses were so popular you saw them everywhere. With their neon frames coming in bright pink, bright green and bright yellow, their darker-than-normal lenses and the tiny "V" logo in the lower corner of the left lens, Vang Sunglasses had put a pretty penny in Tracy's pocket. In my opinion, they weren't the world's best sunglasses— that honor still probably belongs to Ray-Ban—but they were fun and popular, and nobody really cared if their eyes were being protected from UV rays as long as they were fashionable.

I glanced at my watch and noted it was now almost 9:30am. 6:30am in Kauai. Still too early but it wasn't like Tracy was going to answer his own phone anyway. I'm sure he had a butler or an assistant or someone in that big, glorious mansion of his, someone who answered the phone and the door and then announced something along the lines of "Sir, there's a caller for you."

So, I picked up the phone and dialed.

It took a second before the ringing started. Still amazed me that, in this day and age, there was a slight delay in hooking up the mainland with the 50th state. The tone burred twice in my ear, three times, and then an anxious voice came on the line. "Tracy Vang."

Okay, so maybe the butler had the day off.

"Tracy, it's Brace Heller," I said. "Returning your call."

"Oh, thank God, Brace. I'm so glad you called. How've you been?"

"Good, Tracy, I'm good. Yourself?"

"I've been better, Brace. I've been way better. You got my message?"

"I did."

"Malu's in trouble, Brace. Big trouble. Bad trouble. I could really use your help. Can you get out here?"

This didn't sound like the Tracy Vang I knew. The cool and calm businessman who always sported a knowing smile and who was legendary for remaining relaxed in stressful situations. This sounded like a father who would do anything to protect his child and who was at his wit's end to do so.

"Hey, Tracy, slow down a little, okay?" I said. "You know I'm here for you if you need me, but you've got to tell me what's going on."

I heard a pause on the other end, some 2,500 miles away, as Tracy took a deep breath. "Yeah, I'm sorry, Brace. Things are crazy here. Malu's my only son, you know, and with DeeDee gone …"

DeeDee. Vang's high school sweetheart and then wife of almost twenty years. I felt a stab of shame that I'd almost forgotten her. She had passed away from breast cancer only a year or two ago.

"I know, Tracy," I said. "I understand. Now tell me what's going on?"

There was another deep breath. "They say he killed someone, Brace. They say my boy killed someone."

"Who's saying?"

"The cops. They're saying Malu tried to rob the guy and that it went bad. That Malu killed him in an attempt to escape."

"What does Malu say?"

"He says he didn't do it! He didn't, Brace! He couldn't! I know my boy!"

"What kind of evidence do they have?"

Another pause. "Evidence? What are you talking about, Brace? I told you he didn't do it."

"But the cops think he did," I said. "So, tell me, what kind of evidence do they think they have?"

"They say somebody saw him go in the bathroom," Tracy said. "And then come back out. Later, they found the guy dead inside."

"Bathroom?"

"Public bathroom. At one of the beaches."

"So, they have a witness."

"They say they do."

"But no hard evidence, like video or photographs?"

"No, nothing like that. But, Brace, he was there. Malu was in that bathroom."

"Wait. He was?"

"Yes, but he said the guy was alive when he left."

"So, he saw the victim?" I asked.

"He tried to rob him, Brace!" Tracy said, and I heard his voice catch in his throat. "He tried to rob him, but he didn't kill him!"

"Jesus."

"It's this thing …" Tracy started to explain. "Brace, there's too much to talk about. I need you to come out here. Can you? Like today? I'll pay for everything. I'll put you up, give you a retainer, get you a car. Whatever you need! I know it's a lot to ask but I wouldn't be asking if it wasn't so important! If it wasn't my boy!"

I rocked back in my chair, the cell phone pressed to my ear. Marina wasn't going to be happy, but she'd understand. She always did. And, hey, maybe if she can get a few days off, she could come with me, spend a few days in the sunny state of Kauai. But it didn't sound good. In fact, it sounded like Kauai PD had a pretty good case against the son of one of the wealthiest men on the islands.

"I'll work something out," I told Tracy and I could hear his sigh of relief from across the Pacific Ocean. "But I've got to ask you, why isn't this all over the news? Or the web? This is a big story, Tracy, I'm surprised they're not all over you."

"I'm working with the Kauai PD," Tracy said. "I've got a few friends there. They're keeping everything under wraps for now, but they tell me it won't last long. That's why I need you out here now, Brace, the sooner the better." He went quiet for a moment, and I heard what sounded like a choked sob. "Send me all your info via e-mail," he said quietly. "And I'll set up your flight and itinerary. I can't thank you enough for this, Brace. I know it's a lot to ask but you're literally the only person who can help us here."

"I'll do what I can, Tracy," I said. "I'll send you all my information in a second. And I'll see you no later than tomorrow morning."

"Thanks, Brace. Thank you so much."

And the line went dead.

CHAPTER FOUR

As I expected, and because it's one of the reasons I love her, Marina wasn't thrilled that I was jetting off to Kauai the next morning, but she understood why I had to do it.

"Do you think he did it?" she asked me. "Do you think he killed that man?"

"Don't have enough information to be sure," I said. "Unfortunately, it's possible. Tracy flat out admitted that Malu robbed the man, and we all know that robberies sometimes go sour. Maybe he never intended to kill him but maybe things got out of hand. I don't want to say he killed him by accident because he was stupid enough to put himself in that position. But shit happens. It's entirely possible he did."

"But there's also the possibility he didn't."

"There are always possibilities," I said. "And I hope for Tracy's sake Malu didn't kill anybody."

"And Malu's," Marina said.

"Yes," I agreed. "And Malu's."

We were sitting at home, out on the patio, enjoying our Lean Cuisine frozen dinners. Marina was eating rigatoni something or other. I had a Salisbury Steak with Macaroni and Cheese. I would have preferred mashed potatoes, but you can't have everything. It was a cool evening, but not a cold one and the sun had just disappeared beneath the horizon. The cool blue of dusk had become the cobalt of night.

Marina took a nibble of pasta and chewed for a moment. She followed that with a sip of white wine. "How long are you going to be gone?"

I shook my head. "No idea. Could be a few days, could be a few weeks. Depends on how things go." I picked up my glass and had a sip of the Dogfish Head 90 beer inside. "I wish you could get some time off."

"I can't," she said forlornly. "You know how that vacation crap works. Unless I put in for it a year in advance, I'm not going anywhere."

"We really need to win the lottery," I said. "So, we can do whatever we want, whenever we want."

"From your lips to God's ears."

We ate for a few moments in silence.

"So, you and Tracy were good friends in high school?" Marina asked.

I nodded. "Maybe not *best* friends," I said. "But good friends" I laughed softly. "We actually met in Creative Writing class, of all things. Tracy used to write these incredible stories about surfing. I remember one story he wrote about a group of surfer dudes who go to this secret beach in California. They're out there surfing and there's this old man there who's just *shredding* the waves. The kids watch him in awe and finally, when the man comes out of the water and onto the beach, the kids realize it's Richard Nixon … and they're on his private beach."

Marina smiled. "That's funny."

"It is. It was a great story."

"And that's where you knew DeeDee from?"

"Yeah," I said. "DeeDee was in that same class." I frowned. "Don't remember what she wrote, though."

"And they met there?"

"They did. It was one of those high school romances that everyone knew about. You didn't say Tracy without saying DeeDee at the same time. True love, I guess."

"But she died."

"Yeah," I said. "Breast cancer. Very sad. Just goes to show you that no matter how much money you have, there are some things you can't beat."

"Fuckin' cancer," Marina said.

"Fuckin' cancer," I agreed.

Marina drank her wine. I drank my beer. The night grew darker and a little colder around us. Wurzel snored softly beneath the table, confident that the sound of food dropping nearby would wake him instantly and give him time to pounce.

"I'm going to miss you," Marina said.

"I'm going to miss you, too," I said. "I'll be as quick as I can."

"I know you will," she said. "But this is important, Brace. If that kid is innocent, you need to get him out of this."

"Well, he's not *innocent*," I said. "He did admit to trying to rob the guy."

"You know what I mean."

"I do. And, if he didn't kill the guy, I'll help him prove it."

She reached across the table and touched my hand. I looked into her eyes. It would have been a magic moment if Wurzel hadn't chosen that moment to release a high-pitched doggy fart that went on far longer than it should have.

Marina and I laughed until there were tears in our eyes.

Chapter Five

I took the redeye to Kauai, not because it was cheaper (What did I care? Tracy was footing the bill) but because it was the quickest way to get there.

The flight was only half full and the seat beside me was unoccupied, so I was able to spread out a little which I appreciated because I don't like to fly cramped. Not that I would have been cramped anyway. This was the first time I'd flown First Class and it was obscenely spacious. I settled back in my very comfortable seat, powered up my iPad and opened Netflix. All I needed for the rest of my flight were a few Jack and Cokes and my First-Class meal

(which, according to the menu in the seat pocket, was Beef Kare Kare, whatever the hell that was.)

I decided to start my flight with a little information about where we were going. I'd never been to Hawaii before, and therefore not Kauai, so I was glad when I found an article in the in-flight magazine tucked into the seat pocket in front of me entitled KAUAI – ISLAND PARADISE/PARADISE ISLAND. It read:

If your destination is the island of Kauai, you are in for one terrific visit! Kauai, or "The Garden Isle," is one of Hawaii's most amazing and versatile destinations. There is so much to see and do here but, if you'd rather just sit at the beach and read a book, Kauai is laid back enough to let you do exactly just that.

Kauai is geologically the oldest of the main Hawaiian Islands. With an area of just over 562 square miles, it is the fourth largest in the Hawaiian chain. The tropical climate here is generally humid and stable all year round although there can be instances of extreme weather, especially rain. Precipitation in Kauai's mountainous regions averages somewhere between 50 and 100 inches annually, and Mt Wai'ale'ale is often cited as being the wettest place on the planet.

Based on data from 1931 through 2004, the average yearly precipitation there was an astonishing 417 inches.

Like most of the other Hawaiian Islands, Kauai's largest industry is tourism, with well over a million people visiting annually. And those tourists spend close to a billion dollars during their stay there.

Kauai is well-known for its wild chickens, which roam the island everywhere. You'll be able to find plenty of Kauai Chicken merchandise anywhere you go. The chickens arrived with the original Polynesian settlers, who brought them along as food.

If you've never been to Kauai, but get a sense of déjà vu when you arrive, there may be an explanation. Kauai has been featured in almost a hundred Hollywood movies and television shows. The original musical South Pacific was filmed here, and Waimea Canyon was used in Steven Spielberg's blockbuster movie Jurassic Park. Other films shot here include Raiders of the Lost Ark, Six Days, Seven Nights, and the 1976 version of King Kong. The Descendants, starring George Clooney, was filmed in the village of Hanalei and you can actually visit the barstool he frequented at the Tahiti Nui bar there.

If you're a hiking fan, there's nothing like Kauai's hidden trails. You'll visit pristine areas featuring unmatched flora with views that will quite literally take your breath away.

Of course, that's far from all there is to know about Kauai, but it's enough to get you started on your visit to The Garden Isle.

That may have been far from all there is to know about Kauai, but it was all I needed for the moment, so I closed the magazine and tucked it back into the seat pocket. I glanced at my watch. We'd been in the air for about an hour, which meant we had four more hours to go. So far, the flight attendant, who introduced herself as Carrie, had been kind enough to offer me two Jack and Cokes and a hot towel for my face. I accepted the drinks but politely refused the hot towel.

I had downloaded a few movies from Netflix in preparation for the flight. One of them was a documentary on the last tour of Black Sabbath and the others were action/adventure movies, one of them starring Jason Statham and the other with Dwayne Johnson. I chose them because they were all loud and I hoped that the volume would drown out the sounds of the plane crashing nose-first into the Pacific.

The Jack and Cokes had done their job and I was starting to relax. It wasn't that I was afraid of flying, it's just that I don't like the lack of control. Behind the wheel of a car, I can turn or brake to avoid an obstacle in the road. In a plane, you follow the direction the pilot takes you in … no matter what direction that may be.

I screwed my earbuds into my ears, leaned back and brought up the Black Sabbath doc, turning the volume up as loud as I could stand it. I mean, it's Black Sabbath, right?

Sometime later, I awoke to find Carrie standing in the aisle with her back to me and the documentary I'd started watching long over. I was thankful the iPad hadn't clattered to the floor when I dozed off. I closed the tablet and set it on the seat beside me, pulling the buds out of my ears and enjoying the cool clear rush of air into the spaces they'd previously inhabited.

"How are you doing, sir?" Carrie asked and her professional tone made it seem like she really cared. "Comfortable?"

"Very much so," I said. "Fell asleep watching a Black Sabbath documentary."

She nodded in a friendly, off-hand way that told me she had no idea who Black Sabbath were, then knelt down and tugged at a drawer on the cart she was pulling. "You had the Beef Kare Kare, right?"

"Right" I said. "I ordered it because I have no idea what it is."

"Oh, it's good," she said. "It's stewed beef in peanut butter sauce." She placed a bowl of what looked like orange-brown soup in front of me. It was thick with chunks of beef, a leafy vegetable (spinach?) and slices of what were either some type of pepper or cucumbers. A savory aroma floated up off it that made my mouth water. "Some wine with your meal?" Carrie asked.

"No wine," I said. "But I will have another Jack and Coke."

"You mean a Lemmy?"

I blinked, surprised, and gave her a look. She nodded at my battered Motorhead t-shirt.

"My dad was a huge Motorhead fan," she said. "After Lemmy died, dad stopped drinking Jack and Cokes. Well, I mean, he kept drinking them, only he called them Lemmys. That always stuck in my head."

"Yeah, there was a push to start calling them that," I nodded. "Didn't really catch on."

"Too bad."

"Yeah, too bad. Either way, I'll have another one."

"You got it," Carrie said, pushing her cart back toward the station. "I'll be right back with that."

I sampled my Beef Kare Kare. The peanut butter sauce was savory and delicious and the beef tender and juicy. Carrie brought me my next Lemmy and I thanked her.

"How's your Beef Kare Kare?" she asked.

"Wonderful. First time I've had it."

"I'm glad you like it," Carrie said. "Are you headed to Kauai for business or pleasure?"

"Strictly business. Had to leave the wife at home so no pleasure allowed."

Carrie laughed. "What kind of business are you in?"

"I'm a private detective," I said.

"Really?" Carrie's eyebrows arched. "You mean like Magnum P.I.?"

It was my turn to laugh. "Something like that," I said. "Trust me, it's nothing quite so glamorous."

Carrie graced me with another gorgeous smile. "Let me know if you need anything else," she said, and then she and her cart disappeared up the aisle.

I sipped at my Lemmy and finished my Beef Kare Kare and leaned way back in my seat and stretched out my legs. There was plenty of room.

I decided I liked flying First Class, at least as long as people as nice as Carrie were taking care of me.

CHAPTER SIX

Because of the three-hour time difference between Los Angeles and Kauai, it was still just as dark when we arrived as it was when we had departed. I was a little disappointed. I was looking forward to following nothing but the blue carpet of the Pacific beneath me until we arrived at the tiny little island in the middle of nowhere.

Instead, there was nothing outside my window but darkness until we were nearly to the airport. Then, as we descended to the runway, the lights of the city of Lihue began to sparkle beneath us. Compared to L.A., there weren't many of them.

I watched the world slide past beneath me. There was a definitive break where the ocean ended and the shoreline began because the airport was very near the water and the darkness ended suddenly, just as the light began. Off in the near distance was a harbor, an enormous cruise ship resting there, its many thousands of lights either dimmed or turned off as the ocean-bound partiers came home to call it a night. It was nearly 3am, after all. I wondered if it would still be there when the sun came up.

We set down in Lihue with a gentle bump and the plane taxied to a stop. After a few moments, Carrie came down the aisle, thanked us all for flying with Hawaiian Airlines, and reminded us not to forget any of our belongings. I exited the plane, taking a moment to thank the captain for a pleasant flight, something I always try to do. As I walked through the connecting tube to the airport, I felt a stab of guilt for the people still sitting on the plane in coach. *The Peasants*, I thought, thinking of that jerk Lynn Fuller from DiabetiCorp.

Lihue airport is a tiny one, especially in relation to an international airport like Los Angeles or even Burbank, and it only took me a moment to navigate from the departure area to the main lobby. As I walked through the halls, I was surprised to see sheets of rain beating against the windows. Maybe the article I'd read was right. Maybe this was one of the rainiest places on earth. Just my luck: I finally get an all-expenses-paid trip to Hawaii, and they send me to the only island where it rains 24/7.

A sea of tourists stood around a carousel, anxiously watching luggage of various sizes and shapes going round and round and round. Occasionally, one of tourists would leap forward, panther-like, to snag a bag off the belt and then step back to await the next one. No, thank you. Everything I needed was packed in the backpack strapped across my shoulders. It wasn't like I was going to Croatia or some other third world country. If I needed something in Kauai, I'd go to Walmart and buy it. There was no reason I needed to pack thirteen pairs of boxer shorts.

I walked past the carousel and out into the night. Not only was the Lihue airport comparatively small, but it also had an open-air feel to it that I liked. Even though it was now almost 3:30 in the morning, the air felt warm and close, and the humidity was like a living thing, clinging to my body like a wet towel.

A 6 Passenger Lincoln Navigator SUV sat parked at the curb, gleaming in the night despite being pummeled with raindrops the size of fists. On the sidewalk near the car, out of the rain beneath a canopy, stood a giant of a man packed into what looked like an expensive blue suit, its seams tight. He stood at least 6' 6" and had shoulders that seemed very close to that measurement as well. His black hair was combed straight back over his head and down past his shoulders and was glued down with something like Vaseline or superglue. He had Polynesian features and wore a smile that I'm sure he thought were welcoming but instead sent a buzz of raw fear right through me. His shoes were so brightly polished that the few lights set into the overhang reflected off them like Hollywood search lights.

And he was holding a sign that said: HELLER.

I walked over to where he stood and looked up into his face, very much aware of the angle of my head. The man was at least six inches taller than me, but his massive bulk made it feel like even more. I tried to give him a friendly smile but that proved difficult since my thoughts were screaming, *He could tear you apart with his bare hands!*

"I'm Heller," I said. "Brace Heller."

The man's eerie smile immediately brightened into one of genuine friendliness. The transformation was stunning. "Mr. Heller!" he said, and his voice reflected his size, deep and strong and commanding. "My name is Alika, sir, and I am at your service. Mr. Vang sent me." He looked down at my empty hands, puzzled. "You have no luggage, sir?"

"No, no luggage," I said. "Too cumbersome. All I have is this." And I pulled at the straps of the backpack, swinging it forward.

"Let me get that for you, sir," said Alika, snatching up the bag as though it was filled with someone's sack lunch for the day, not their clothes for a week. "Our car is right here."

He led me to the rear passenger door, my backpack looking like a toy in a giant's hand, and opened it for me. He used his massive palm to guide me in and tucked me nicely in the backseat, closing the door with a crash that sounded like it would knock it off its hinges. He tossed the backpack in the trunk, came around and sat in the driver's seat. The Lincoln started up like a champ and the next thing I knew we were on our way.

"Thanks for picking me up, Alika," I said. "I didn't expect it to be so wet here."

Alika gave a little chuckle. "Actually, sir, it's usually very wet here. It rains a lot here in Kauai. We are very pleased when we actually get some sun."

"Really? That much?"

Alika laughed again. "No, not really. But it does rain here a lot. If you're looking for sun, especially at the beach, I recommend Poipu. *Sunny Poipu*, we call it. When the rest of Kauai is raining, Poipu usually has some sun."

"Good to know," I said. "So, Tracy asked you to pick me up?"

"Yes, sir," Alika said. "He told me you are a V.I.P. and to take very good care of you."

"Well, I don't know about that."

"If Mr. Vang says you are a V.I.P., you are a V.I.P.," Alika said.

"How long have you worked for him?"

"Eleven years," Alika said. "First as security, then as his personal driver."

"That's a long time," I said.

"Yes, sir," Alika said. "And I am grateful for every moment."

"Please, call me Brace."

"Thank you, Brace. I am pleased to meet you."

"So where are we off to? I assume we're not meeting with Tracy and Malu at this hour."

"No, sir," Alika said. "Mr. Vang said you would be very tired from your flight. He asked that I take you to your residence, to make sure you get settled in and then to let you rest. He asked that you meet him this morning at 9am, at his residence."

I glanced at my watch. It was nearly four. I wouldn't get much sleep, but I knew how important this was to Tracy. "That'll work," I said. "I am a little tired. How long until we arrive at ... um, the residence?"

"About fifty minutes," Alika said. "Mr. Vang has put you up at The Cliffs Resort in Princeville. Very nice place. You will love it. Two stories, two full bedrooms, a kitchen, and a lanai that overlooks the ocean." He grinned and looked over his shoulder at me. "Mr. Vang sent my *Ku'uipo* and I there last year for our anniversary. It was wonderful."

"Good to know," I said.

We drove on for a few moments in silence. I noticed that we seemed to have slipped away from the city. Gone were the Burger Kings and Walmarts and in their place was mostly darkness.

Alika seemed to sense my thoughts. "Might I recommend, sir …"

"Brace. Please."

"Might I recommend, Brace, that you sit back, relax and perhaps even take a little nap? I'll get you there safely."

I had just met Alika and knew virtually nothing about him. Yet, I sensed that he was telling the truth. He *would* get me there safely. Because he had been charged with doing so by Tracy Vang and he did not want to disappoint him.

"Thanks, Alika. I think I'll do that."

And I wriggled back into the leather seat and closed my eyes just to rest them.

CHAPTER SEVEN

The Cliffs was even better than Alika had described. It was a collection of condominium style vacation homes that were perched, as the name promised, near the edge of a cliff below which rolled the vast Pacific Ocean. Alika carried my backpack up the flight of stairs to the second floor and opened the door with a plastic card key. He stood back and allowed me to enter, telling me gently, "Your shoes, sir. Please remove them. It's tradition here."

I peeled back the Velcro strap on my Tevas and dropped them on the porch in front of the door. Alika nodded with appreciation. I stepped inside.

It took me a moment to get my bearings. The "residence" was probably half again as big as my small home in Ventura. I was standing in the living room, judging from the giant flatscreen TV and L shaped couch there. Behind me was a master bedroom with a cavernous ceiling, edged with glass windows. Directly in front of me was a sliding glass door leading out to the lanai, complete with a wicker dining table and four wicker chairs. The kitchen was just to the left of that and to the left of the kitchen was a stairway that led to what I assumed was the second-floor bedroom.

"This place is *huge*," I said.

"Yes, and very nice," Alika said. "They are vacation condos usually used as time-shares and they are highly sought after."

"I bet they are. It's beautiful, Alika," I said. "If you see Tracy before I do, please express my thanks to him."

"From what I understand, sir," Alika said. "It is Mr. Vang who thanks you."

"Here, let me take that." I reached for my backpack and Alika passed it to me effortlessly.

"Is there anything I can get for you before I go, sir?" Alika asked. "You'll find that the refrigerator is fully stocked and there is plenty of food in the cupboards." He smiled. "And Mr. Vang said to help yourself to the adult beverages."

I returned the smile and wandered into the kitchen. On the counter, I found a fresh bottle of Maker's Mark and in the refrigerator was a case of Coke Zero and another of Stone IPA.

I looked at Alika curiously. "I haven't spoken to Tracy in nearly twenty years," I said. "How'd he know these were my favorites?"

"He is Tracy Vang," Alika shrugged. "It is his business to know things."

I nodded and closed the refrigerator. "It's almost dawn," I said. "You must be anxious to get home to your wife."

"No wife," Alika told me. "But I do have a wonderful girl waiting for me at home."

"Then allow me to thank you and send you on your way," I said. "I assume you'll pick me up for the meeting?"

"Yes, sir," Alika said. "8:30 okay for you?"

"I'll make it work."

"Sleep well, sir."

"Good night," I said. "Or I guess good morning."

As Alika closed the door behind him, I grabbed the bottle of Maker's Mark and a highball glass and padded onto the lanai. The weather was still warm, although a cool breeze trickled gently through the many palm trees on the property. I sat down and stared out at the black sea, wondering what incredible things might be happening beneath that carpet of endlessly undulating ocean and then turned my mind to business.

I peeled the wax seal from the bottle, spun off the lid and poured myself two fingers. As I sipped, I mused over my schedule. First, I would meet with Tracy, briefly hash over old times, and then sit down and talk with his son, Malu. If the boy were innocent of murder, I would help him prove it. If he was guilty, he was on his own. I was hoping it was the former, for Tracy's sake, if nothing else.

After another glass of bourbon, I felt my eyelids growing almost impossibly heavy, so I capped the bottle, went back in through the sliding glass door, and headed for the large bedroom.

The long day had taken its toll on me and, in mere moments, I was sound asleep.

CHAPTER EIGHT

In the few short hours of sleep I managed, the world had changed around me.

I awoke at eight, took a quick shower, towel-dried my hair and dressed quickly. I grabbed a Coke Zero from the fridge, slipped my Teva's back on, snatched the card key off the counter and closed the door behind me. As I fully expected, Alika was already downstairs, leaning casually against the Lincoln with his arms crossed and an inscrutable look on his face. When he caught sight of me, his smile brightened and he pushed away from the car, opened the rear passenger door, and beckoned me inside. I stopped at the curb and glanced around.

On the way in last night, I had seen only darkness and shadows (when I wasn't napping). There weren't many streetlights in this part of Kauai, and I could only remember the late-night journey into Princeville in shades of blue and black. Today, it seemed as if God had turned on the lights.

The sun was bright and playful, the sky the clearest shade of blue I'd ever seen. The air smelled faintly of the sea, and someone nearby was frying bacon. An odd combination but surprisingly pleasant. Brightly colored birds sang joyfully, flitting around with dreams of breadcrumbs dancing in their heads. Every once in awhile, a rooster belted out a boastful crow. The ground was covered with green everywhere—from the lush lawns growing around the various buildings to the hundreds of palm trees sprouting up virtually everywhere. I had heard that palm trees weren't native to Hawaii but, hot damn, these days you couldn't see one without thinking about the place. Well, that and California, I guess.

I looked up at Alika and nodded. "So, this is why they call it paradise, eh?"

He smiled warmly. "I call it home."

"You're a lucky man." I hopped in the back of the Lincoln and Alika closed the door. A moment later, he climbed into the driver's seat, and we were off.

We drove through an impressive collection of resorts and hotels, all of them boasting lavish architecture and lush landscaping. We passed a golf course, its sprawling green carpet dotted with carts and players carrying clubs. Finally, we hit Highway 56 and Alika took a left, heading south. We drove another ten minutes through towering walls of jungle growth and the occasional waterfall, and then turned left again at a sign reading Pila'a Beach.

The road got sketchier the farther we got in. It went from government asphalt to consumer cement to rough gravel in a very short period. Alika glanced over his shoulder at one point and said, "Sorry. Mr. Vang hasn't gotten around to fixing up this part of the road yet."

"No worries."

We came to a giant iron gate that was met at both sides with a high, red-brick wall that stretched each way as far as I could see. Alika reached up to the visor and pulled out a tiny remote control. He hit a button and the gates split apart, rumbling open. Alika put the remote back and we drove through.

The gates led to a pebbled roadway, lined on each side by impossibly luxuriant grass, that took us to the main house. It wasn't as enormous as I expected but the word "mansion" still applied. As we neared the rolling stone stairs that spilled out from what was apparently the front doorway, I caught a glimpse of Tracy Vang in the flesh for the first time in nearly twenty years. He didn't look much different from the photos I'd seen on Facebook, Instagram, and every damn where else.

Tracy stood on the porch in his usual uniform: A pair of weather-beaten blue jeans, a black t-shirt adorned with a tribal design, and a pair of lime green FlipFlat sandals, a brand he had designed, that glowed in the tropical sunlight like the moon does at midnight. He also sported a pair of dark sunglasses with frames that matched the color of his shoes.

You couldn't see his eyes behind the dark lenses but the smile on his well-tanned face told you all you needed to know. It was the trademarked Vang grin that had brought laughs and joy to millions around the world (and millions of dollars to Tracy's bank account) but it was uncharacteristically rounded at the edges with what I could only assume were weariness and worry.

As Alika brought the Lincoln to a stop, Tracy came down the stairs and opened the door for me. "Brace Heller, as I live and breathe!" he bellowed, swallowing me in an irresistible bear hug the moment I got to my feet. "I can't tell you how thankful I am you came out here," he whispered in my ear. "Thank you, old friend."

"Who the fuck you calling old?" I told him, breaking the hug and holding him at arm's distance. I gave him an appraising look. "Holding up pretty well for your age, aren't you?"

"You're one to talk," Tracy said, clapping my shoulder. "How the hell you been, Brace?"

"Been well," I said. "Life is good."

"It is, isn't it?" Tracy asked with another dash of sadness in his voice. "Come on in, Brace. Let's have a beer and catch up." He turned his attention to Alika. "That's all for now, Alika. Thank you."

"Of course, sir," Alika replied, climbing back into the SUV, and driving away.

"That's a good guy you've got there," I told Tracy.

"Alika? The best. Been with me forever."

Tracy guided me through the front door. "God, it's good to see you," he said. "How was your flight? Your accommodations okay?"

"Okay?" I asked. "They're opulent. You own that place?"

Tracy shook his head. "No, no, no. Just the one condo. The others are mostly timeshares although a couple of them have year-round residents."

He led me through a long hallway that led through the house to an outside patio area. "I'll give you the grand tour later," he said. "Like I said, I thought we'd just sit, have a brew, and talk about the world."

We passed through a screen door and onto a wooden deck overlooking a verdant jungle that angled out away from the home where it tumbled into the sea. The waves crashed gently on the rocks below us and I could easily imagine being lulled to sleep by their gentle soothing sound.

Tracy seemed to read my thoughts. "Yeah, it's nice now," he said. "But when we get a storm, which happens more often than I'd like, it gets downright scary out here."

"I bet it does."

"You want a beer?"

"Sure, what have you got?"

"You name it, I've probably got it. Keep a pretty good cellar downstairs."

I laughed. "How is it you never wound up in the craft beer business?" I asked. "Seems like it'd be right up your alley."

Tracy smirked. "You'd think," he said. "But the risk versus reward was never too enticing to me. By the time craft beer broke big, it was too late."

"A dollar short and a day late," I said.

"Well," Tracy said, giving me a playfully smug smile. "A day late, maybe."

I decided to test Tracy's beer I.Q. and asked him if he had any Dogfish Head and off he went to search the cellar. While he was gone, I texted Marina to let her know that I missed her and that I would call her later. When Tracy returned, I was delighted to see that he had two bottles of Dogfish Head 90-Minute IPA. I admitted I was impressed.

We talked about old times, re-told decades old stories, and reminisced about old friends. We talked about how much we both missed DeeDee, and I lamented the fact that I had barely spoken to her after the wedding. Tracy asked about Marina and even Wurzel which once again led me to wonder exactly how much research he had done. And then I realized it wasn't research at all.

It was social media.

Tracy finished his beer and wiggled the empty bottle at me. I nodded. "Maybe not a 90," I told him. "Those pack a kick and I've got work to do."

He was gone and back in about three minutes, this time with a pair of Bikini Blonde Lagers from Maui Brewing Company. He handed one to me and we popped the tops and clinked the cans together ceremoniously. Tracy fell back into his chair.

Finally, the topic of Malu came around.

"Malu's been a little out of sorts ever since DeeDee died," he started. "It wasn't anything major, at first. Trouble in school, bad grades, mostly. And then a couple of fights. It wasn't easy but I kept him in school long enough to graduate…"

"Jesus, he's graduated high school?" I said, incredulous. "How fucking old are we?"

"Pretty fucking old," Tracy laughed. "Yeah, he graduated back in June, four months ago. Graduated with a D but at least he got his diploma." He took a sip of beer. "Anyway, it was when school was over that things got really dicey. He started keeping really weird hours, even for a kid. I mean, he'd sleep till noon or one, get up, have some breakfast, and then disappear until the wee hours of the morning, I'm talking like four or five AM. He was always sleepy and irritable, at least to me. I just didn't get it."

"Drugs?" I asked quietly.

"Well, yeah," Tracy said. "But nothing dangerous. He just became … well, a *pothead*. All he wanted to do all day was smoke weed and watch TV. That is, when he was home, which was basically never."

"Which is all *you* wanted to do when you were his age as I remember," I said.

"Well, yeah, Brace. That's what we did back then. And I get that's what he wants to do now." He picked up his beer and held it to his forehead. "But then I fucked things up."

"How?" I said.

"I wanted him to get on track," Tracy said. "I wanted him to get his life in order, get a job, *do* something other than smoke weed with his loser friends and play fucking *Call of Duty* all day. So, I cut him off. I stopped giving him his allowance. I mean, shit, he was blowing it all on weed anyway."

"Tough love."

"Well, as tough as I can get," Tracy said. "I mean, he's my only son, Brace, hell, my only *family* now. But I told him he wasn't getting any more money from me until he got his act together."

"And that's why he robbed that man?" I asked. "He needed money for drugs ... or whatever."

"That's part of the reason," Tracy said. "Hell, I guess that's *all* of the reason. His circle of friends got ... well, they went from *losers* to *scumbags* in like two weeks. One week, they were all sitting around with stupid smiles on their faces and empty bags of Flamin' Hot Cheetos on their laps and the next week they were, I don't know ... *different*. It was weird, man. It was like they went from stupid kids to filthy criminals in the course of a few days."

"What do you mean by 'criminals'?" I asked.

"They got all serious," Tracy said. "And dark. I mean, their personalities changed. They got quiet and mean. I'm telling you it was freaky, man."

I took a sip of my beer and leaned in close. "And you think this led to the robbery?"

"I know it did," Tracy said. He reached over to the other side of the table and grabbed a stack of folded newspapers there. He dug through them for a moment and then pushed one over to me. *The Garden Island.* The headline read: PANTS-DOWN BANDITS STRIKE LYDGATE BEACH.

I glanced up at Tracy. He shook his head angrily.

"I know, I know," he said. "Your first reaction is to laugh. That's everyone's first reaction. But I'm telling you, Brace, it isn't funny." He grabbed the newspaper and pulled it back toward him. "This is the group Malu got mixed up in. A group of punks, a gang, basically, who were robbing tourists in public restrooms."

"That's where the 'pants-down' comes from? Like, that's how they wear their pants?"

Tracy hung his head in shame. "Only partly," he said. "They had a strategy, if you can believe it. They'd wait until some tourist went up to the urinal and had his pants around his ankles or his hands on his dick or something, and then they'd pull his pants down and take his wallet at the same time. While the poor sap is trying to keep his pants on, they're running out the door with his cash and credit cards."

I said nothing.

"Don't you see?" Tracy pleaded. "They struck when someone was at their most vulnerable. When they were standing at a urinal, taking a piss, and the only thing on their mind is where they're going to get their Mai Tais tonight."

"Other than the obvious," I said. "Was anybody else ever hurt?"

"Sprains and bruises, maybe," Tracy said. "But mostly it was just humiliating."

"That and the cash, of course."

Tracy nodded. "And the credit cards," he said.

I reached for the newspaper and Tracy slid it back to me. "Apparently, they did this often enough for the newspaper to give them a name," I said.

"They robbed thirteen people over the course of two weeks," Tracy said quietly.

I raised my eyebrows. "When did you realize Malu was involved?"

"Not until the day they say he killed that guy," Tracy told me. "When they called me and told me he was in custody. I swear I had no idea before that."

"How was the guy killed?"

"They say someone …" his voice caught. "They say Malu bashed the back of his head in with a rock."

I screwed up my eyes. "Doesn't sound like their M.O." I said.

"No, it doesn't," Tracy agreed.

I picked up the newspaper and tossed it on the stack of others on the table by Tracy. "I'm gonna want to read these," I said. "But not before I talk to Malu. I want to hear his version before I get the paper's."

"Can't trust the media, right?" Tracy said.

"It's not really that," I said. "But it *is* like a game of Telephone. You remember Telephone?"

"Sure," Tracy said. "You whisper something in a person's ear, and they pass it on to another person. Pretty soon, after they message has been transmitted through like, thirty people, it bears no resemblance to the message you started out with."

"Exactly," I said. "It's human nature. You hear one thing, you can't help but put your mark on it. I want to talk to Malu before I get any pre-conceptions of what went down that night."

"So, when do you want to talk to him?"

"When's the soonest I can?"

"Soon," Tracy said. "Today. But there's someone I want you to meet first."

"Okay."

Tracy glanced at his watch. Its band was nearly as neon as his sunglasses. "A friend of the family," Tracy said. "A cop. I figured you might need a liaison here, so I called in some favors. He's supposed to be here in ten minutes or so."

"Okay," I said again.

"His name's Jay, Jay Huihui. Look, I know your P.I. ticket isn't exactly valid in Kauai."

"That can be debated."

"But it doesn't matter. Jay called in a few favors and you're free to do your thing here. Your license has been expanded to include Kauai. Plus, I figured you might need some help pulling drivers' licenses or running license plates. You know. That sort of thing."

"Watch a lot of TV, do we?"

"What? You won't need those things?

"Maybe, maybe not." I said.

"Okay," Tracy said, looking puzzled. "So, what *do* you need?"

"I need a car," I said. "And a gun."

"A gun?"

"Couldn't exactly bring mine over on the plane," I said.

"No, of course not. And the Lincoln is yours, by the way. Alika will take you anywhere you want."

"I appreciate that," I said. "But I need something a little more subtle, a little more *local*. Something that people won't look twice at."

"Oh, I gotcha," Tracy said, and snapped his fingers. "I think I've got just the thing."

"And the gun?"

"Let's talk to Jay about that."

"You want to talk to a cop about getting me a gun?"

"He'll know what to do," Tracy said. "Like I said, he's *ohana*, a member of the family."

We sat and drank our beers for a few moments, enjoying the smooth lager refreshment. Sure enough, a few moments later, Jay Huihui came walking down the hallway and joined us on the patio outside.

CHAPTER NINE

Jay Huihui the cop was probably half the size of Alika the chauffer, although they shared what looked like the exact same build. He wore a new white t-shirt, the sleeves almost bursting from the powerful biceps swelling beneath them, a pair of tight designer blue jeans and plain black sneakers. There was a small bone earring in his left ear lobe, and I could see the edges of a tribal tattoo reaching up from his collar. I was certain that tattoo went from the middle of his neck to the middle of his chest, essentially covering half of his torso.

Jay stepped out onto the deck and Tracy rose and enveloped him in one of those patented bear hugs. Throughout the embrace, Jay's eyes were locked on me. I couldn't tell if he were sizing me up or just curious about the newcomer, but I got the distinct impression he didn't think I should be there. But maybe I was just telling myself an ugly story.

After a moment, Tracy released him and turned back to me.

"Brace, I'd like you to meet my friend Jay Huihui," he said. "Jay, this is Brace Heller."

We shook hands and I was impressed not only by the strength of Jay's grip, but by the size of his palms. I had big hands but Jay's enveloped mine like a larger size of glove.

"Good to meet you, Mr. Heller," Jay said. "Tracy's told me a lot about you."

"Don't believe everything you hear," I said. "Nice to meet you, too. And, by the way, it's Brace. You know what they say. Mr. Heller was my dad."

Jay laughed. "I've heard that before," he said. "So, you'd better call me Jay, too."

"Deal."

"Gentlemen, please, sit," Tracy said, motioning toward our chairs. "Jay, can I get you something? Coffee? A beer?"

"I'm good," Jay said. "But thanks."

"So, Jay," I said. "Tracy tells me you're a Kauai PD detective."

Jay pursed his lips. "That's right," he said. "Been a cop here on the island for just over five years."

"Born here?"

"Yes, sir," Jay said, and his pride was apparent. "Lived here my whole life. Only left long enough to finish my schooling in Honolulu, and to take a week of vacation in Las Vegas a couple of years ago."

"I've read that a lot of Kauai residents like to go to Las Vegas for vacation," I said. "It's one of my favorite places, too."

"Tracy tells me you were never a cop," Jay said. "Went straight into the P.I. business."

"That's true," I said. "Thought about being a cop, but I didn't like the thought of all that paperwork. We private dicks pretty much get to choose how much paperwork we get to do."

"I hear that," Jay said. He sat forward on the edge of his chair and his face turned serious. "But I gotta be honest. I don't have a lot of faith in gumshoes. Especially gumshoes that have never been on the beat."

Out of the corner of my eye, I saw Tracy give me a worried glance. I held eye contact with Jay and nodded. "I get that," I said. "But it was my understanding that we weren't here to whip out our dicks and a ruler. I thought we were working together to prove Malu Vang was innocent of murder."

Jay stared at me silently for a moment and then his eyes flicked at Tracy. "You're right," he said. "I'm sorry. Tracy told me you're a good guy and that should be enough for me. It's just a little hard for a zebra to change his stripes."

"No harm, no foul," I said. "We're all on the same team here. Which brings me to this: Tracy tells me you can help me find a gun."

Jay's eyebrows came down hard and he looked at Tracy incredulously. "I don't know where you got that impression …" he started.

"I said we'd *talk* to him," Tracy said, looking at me.

"Look," I told both of him. "I have a license to carry in virtually every state but Hawaii. I never thought to get one here because, really, who wants to bring a gun to paradise? But here's the thing. Somebody killed this man in a public bathroom and none of us at this table want to believe it's Malu. Which means it's someone else. Which means I'm going to be out looking for the real murderer, stirring things up, peeking under rocks. I wouldn't investigate this case in California without a gun on me and I'm not about to investigate anything here without a little protection."

"Fine," Jay said, standing. "Then hop on the plane and head back to the mainland. I don't know who you think you are, but we don't need you out here. We've got this completely under control. The only reason I agreed to this meeting was because Tracy and I are old friends. I don't know you from Adam. You think I'm going to give you a gun just because you say you need one? I'd sooner give a gun to Malu."

"Then give it to Malu," I said. "And I'll borrow it from him."

Jay's face twisted with anger and his hands turned into fists at his sides. He opened his mouth to fire back at me when Tracy's quiet voice intervened.

"Jay, get him a gun," Tracy said. "If he says he needs one, he needs one." He held up a flattened palm as Jay began to protest. "I've known him since high school, Jay. He's not going to use that gun unless he has to. If he says he needs it to protect himself, then that's what he needs it for." He paused and looked at Jay meaningfully. "Would you go out and investigate this without your weapon? Would you, Jay?"

Jay shot a glance at Tracy, and then turned his attention back to me, staring hard, vibrating with anger and indecision. Finally, he took a deep breath and sat down.

"All right," he said after a moment. "I'll get him a gun. But you're going to be responsible for it, Tracy, and for him. I don't like the idea of some *haole* running around with a gun, especially a gun I gave him."

Tracy looked at Jay and smiled gently. "He's not a *haole*," he said. "He's *ohana*."

"If you say so," Jay said, but his eyes made it clear he still wasn't 100% sold. "I'll see what I can dig up, drop it by tomorrow."

"I appreciate that, Jay," I said, with a comforting smile. "Now, tell me about this Pants Down gang."

"Stupid newspaper," Jay said, and I could sense him relaxing a little. "Got names for everything." He sniffed absently. "The Pants Down gang is a group of stoners who ran out of money and couldn't support their habit."

"Addicts?"

"No, just pot. And, as I'm sure you know, pot isn't addictive. But people sure seem to take to it. This particular group of potheads, there was about ten of them, never had any problem scoring their dope because one of them always had money."

"Malu," Tracy said sadly.

"Yes, Malu," Jay said, and his voice echoed the sadness of Tracy's. "Tracy is a wealthy man, and he gave his son a substantial ... I guess you'd call it *allowance*. It was easy for Malu and his friends to find what they were looking for ... especially on this island."

"Pot a big cash crop here on Kauai?"

"Where isn't it?"

"Point taken," I said. "Then what happened?"

"The money dried up," Jay said, and I saw Tracy look away out of the corner of my eye. "Tracy stopped paying Malu his allowance and his team of miscreants decided they had to find another way to make money to score their weed. I don't know which one had the bright idea, but they turned to robbery. Specifically, robbery in public bathrooms when their targets had their pants down to take a leak."

"Easy marks," I said, and Jay nodded his agreement. "And they got away with this for a couple of weeks?"

"Yes," Jay said. "And they probably would have gotten away with it longer if the newspaper hadn't picked up on it. Gave them that ridiculous name. Those articles led to public outcry which led to greater police involvement which led to our arresting Malu at Lydgate Beach."

I held up my hand. "I'd rather forego the official explanation at the moment, if you don't mind," I said. I saw Jay bristle, so I quickly clarified. "I haven't had the opportunity to speak with Malu yet and I'd like to hear it from him first. I'm sure you understand." I leaned forward, drained the rest of my beer, and turned my attention to Tracy.

"So, when can I talk to Malu?" I asked.

"Today," he said. "Hell, now, if you'd like."

"He's here?"

"Yeah, yeah," Tracy said. "Up in his bedroom, probably playing some damn videogame or watching Netflix. He's been grounded since I bailed him out of jail."

"Grounded?" I asked. "How's that working out?"

"Have you seen the size of Alika?" Jay asked. "Malu's not going anywhere."

I nodded. "So, let's got have a chat."

Tracy dropped his beer on a cardboard coaster and pushed back away from the table. "Come on," he said. "I'll introduce you to my son."

Chapter Ten

Malu's bedroom was almost as big as my entire house. It was a cavernous space with an enormous bed in one corner, a computer desk against one wall and an entertainment center, complete with a giant flat-screen TV, against another. The walk-in closet was as big as my kitchen. Posters of such rock bands as Linkin Park and Oasis adorned the walls. There was a Black Sabbath and Marilyn Manson poster as well. Malu apparently had quite a varied taste in music.

And he was apparently a musician, too. A Sunburst Gibson Les Paul hung on one of those wall hooks that musicians use … not the plastic display case of a collector.

Malu looked up at us from where he was sitting cross-legged on the bed. He appeared calm and collected but there was something else there as well. A look that told me he knew he was in trouble and that he had a faint tinge of hope that maybe we could get him out of it.

He scrambled off the bed, dropped the tablet he'd been perusing on the mattress, and came toward us. He was taller than Tracy, I noticed, and not nearly as well-built. Thinner. His long black hair fell just past his shoulders, and he had what looked like a three-day growth of beard shadowing his lower jaw. He wore a Danzig *Circle of Snakes* t-shirt and a pair of well-worn board shorts. His feet were bare.

"Malu, this is Brace Heller, the friend I told you about," Tracy said. "Brace, this is my son, Malu."

I took another step toward Malu and he met me halfway, arm outstretched, ready to greet me. He looked me in the eyes as we shook hands (his grip was firm and confident) and then stood back and crossed his arms.

"My dad says you're a detective," Malu said.

"Your dad is right," I said. "I've been a private investigator for a long, long time."

"Are you going to help me?" Malu asked.

"Yes," I told him flatly. "As long as you're honest with me."

"I will be," Malu said. "I promise."

And I sort of believed him.

Tracy pulled some chairs together and we sat, Malu perching on the edge of the bed. It was quiet in the room for a moment.

"So, you're into Danzig," I said, nodding at Malu's t-shirt.

Malu gave me an unsure smile. "I'm into all kinds of music," he said. "But, yeah, I like Danzig."

I nodded at his t-shirt again. "Not their best album," I said. "I prefer the first one."

Malu's smile became more of a grin. "Yeah," he said simply.

"I worked for him on the *Black Laden Crown* tour," I said. "He was having some trouble with some far-right religious group and had received a few death threats. The record company hired a bunch of additional security, and I was on one of the teams." I laughed at the memory. "Stood off to the side of the stage for most of that tour," I said. "The things going on in that audience ... Well, let's just say it got a little wild."

"I can imagine," Malu said, his eyes wide with interest.

"Maybe I'll sit down and tell you about them sometime," I said. "When we have less important things to discuss."

Malu nodded sadly. "That would be cool," he said quietly.

"So, Malu. I want you to tell me what happened that night."

He closed his eyes and sighed. "I already told the police," he said. "Over and over again."

"I know," I said. "But you haven't told me."

Malu nodded again. "Okay," he said. He wiggled around on the bed, re-settling himself, and then looked up at me. "We were all sitting around with nothing to do …"

"Sitting around *where*, Malu?"

"Over at the farm," Malu said. "Out by where the pigs are."

"There's a farm not too far from here," Tracy clarified. "Big green pastures full of cows and pigs and chickens. Kids go hang out there sometimes, just to have someplace to go."

"Okay," I said. "So, you were sitting around at the farm with nothing to do …"

"Yeah," Malu continued. "And then someone goes, 'why don't we go get some weed?' And I was, like, 'cause we don't have any money. And they were all trying to get me to go get some money from my dad or something and I told him I couldn't do that anymore." He paused and took a deep, measured breath. "And so, then they said, 'you know what that means,' and I knew what that means … uh, meant. That meant we were going to get some money, like we had before."

"By robbing tourists," I said.

Malu shrugged and looked down at the bed shameful-ly. "It works," he said. "Those tourists always carry too much money. We rob one, we got weed for a few days. And it wasn't like it was dangerous or anything. I mean, we figured how can they come after us if their pants are down?"

"Entrepreneurial," I said.

Malu snapped his fingers and pointed at me as though I'd just won some prize. "Right," he said. "So, we all climbed into Hilo's van and …"

"Who's Hilo?" I asked.

"Hilo," Malu said, as if I should know. "He's like my best friend."

I glanced over at Tracy who clandestinely rolled his eyes.

"So, you all hopped into Hilo's van …" I prompted.

"We all hopped in the van and headed over to Lyd-gate Beach," Malu said.

"Why Lydgate Beach?" I asked.

"Because there's always families there," he said. "Dads in swim trunks always stuff their wallet into those tiny pockets and most of the time they're like hanging half out. Easy to get at."

"Okay," I said. "So, you got to Lydgate beach. Then what?"

"So, we got there and parked near the exit, so we could jet real fast after we scored. And me and Hilo went into the men's bathroom and waited."

"Just waited?" I said, imagining what other trouble two naïve teenagers could get into standing around in a public bathroom.

"Yeah, just waited," Malu said. "For the right guy to come in. Somebody not too big and who looked like they had money. And sure enough, in walks this guy."

"Tell me about him," I said.

Malu stared at me uncertainly.

"You know," I clarified. "What'd he look like? What was he wearing? How'd he walk? Had you seen him before? Anything."

"Um, no, I hadn't seen him before," Malu said. "He was just some guy, some dude in flowery trunks and one of those loud Aloha shirts. But his wallet was practically *falling* out of his pocket, and we could tell by the way he rushed in that he really had to go."

"Was he wearing sunglasses?" I asked.

Malu gave me another one of those confused looks. "I don't know," he said. "I don't remember. What difference does that make?"

"Maybe none," I said. "Go on."

"So, we waited until he walked up to the urinal and, you know, whipped out his dick. And then Hilo ran up behind him and yanked his trunks all the way down while I grabbed his wallet."

"What did he do?"

"All he could do. He yelled and cussed and tried to pull up his pants to chase after us. But he couldn't. We knew that. We'd done this before."

"What did you do next?"

"We got the hell out of there," Malu said. "Hilo and I ran out, laughing our asses off, and jumped into the van. We peeled out of there and jetted back up to Kapa'a to score some weed."

"So," I said, "When you left, the gentleman you robbed was still very much alive."

"Yes!" Malu said, bouncing on the edge of the bed and nodding furiously. "Yes, he was still alive! I swear to God! I never even touched him!"

"Was there anybody else in the bathroom?" I asked.

"No, just me, Hilo and that dude."

"No one in the stalls?"

"No," Malu said. "We looked. We didn't want anyone to see us."

I tried to visualize the scene in my mind. It seemed clear enough.

"How'd they finger you?" I said. "What led the cops to you?"

Malu shrugged. I glanced up at Huihui.

"Eyewitness," he said. "Guy saw them coming out of the bathroom before we found the victim."

"Timeline fit?"

Jay nodded. "Close enough."

"How long had the guy been dead before the body was discovered?"

"Not long," Jay said. "Twenty minutes, maybe half an hour."

"And your witness didn't see anyone else come out or go into the bathroom in that time?"

Jay shook his head. "Nope," he said. "And he was right there playing volleyball with his friends the whole time."

"Did the other players see anything?"

Jay shook his head.

"So, they could have easily missed someone else going in and coming out," I said. "In the heat of the game, right?"

"Could have," Jay said. "But when you go into a public bathroom and find a dead body and the last thing anyone saw was these two idiots running out of there as fast as they could, you tend to make a connection."

"Plus, they had the wallet."

"Plus, they had the wallet," Jay admitted.

"But that doesn't mean they murdered someone."

"We didn't!" Malu chirped.

"No," Jay admitted again. "It does not."

I thought for a moment. "Any chance I can talk to this eyewitness?" I asked.

Jake shook his head. "Nope. Not a chance in hell."

"Figured. How about this Hilo?"

"If you can find him," Jay said. "He took a powder once we arrested Malu. Nobody has seen him since."

"Why am I not surprised? And how about the victim? Who was he?"

Tracy stood and gave a meaningful nod toward Malu. "Hey, guys," he said to me and Jay. "Maybe we should go in the other room and talk about this."

"No," I said. "We'll talk right here," I said. "Whether he killed anyone or not, Malu is a part of this. He's the reason we're all here. We need him to be in the loop whether it's uncomfortable for him or not."

Tracy gave me a look that made me believe he was going to challenge me. "Okay," he said after a moment, and sat back down. "That makes sense."

"So, tell me about the victim," I asked again.

"His name was Matt Akana," Jay said. "Forty-nine years old, married, has three kids, all of whom live here in

Kauai. Akana was a real estate agent, had an office up in Princeville. He dealt mostly with commercial properties but sold a house here and there. Mostly ultra-wealthy clients, as you can imagine. There isn't any cheap real estate left in Kauai anymore. I know he represented a few celebrities, a few dot.com rich. And I know he made a ton of moolah. As far as we can tell, he was returning from showing a property near the airport in Lihue and stopped on the way to take a leak."

"Picked the wrong fucking place to take a leak," I said. "Wrong place, wrong time."

"I swear I didn't kill him, Mr. Heller," Malu said quietly. I turned to look at him and was surprised to see that he'd curled up on his bed in a fetal position and had his hand up over his mouth. His eyes were dark and haunted, and it seemed as though he couldn't close them. He just stared out into space, as though contemplating his future, a future that had all but been erased by one simple act.

"If you didn't kill him, Malu, I will help you prove it," I said. "But you've got to be honest with me. You've got to tell me everything, answer any question I ask." I stood up and walked over to him, staring down at him curled up on the bed. "Can you do that?" I asked.

He merely nodded silently, his eyes never moving away from whatever he was staring off into.

"Malu, I need to talk to Hilo," I said. "Do you know where he is?"

Malu just stared at me, but his eyes flicked over to Jay.

"I need to talk to him," I said again. "Do you think you can arrange that?"

"You want to talk to Hilo?" he asked, looking up at me after a moment.

"I do," I said. "Can you work that out?"

His eyes flicked toward Jay again.

"It'll be just me and Hilo," I said, throwing Jay a meaningful glance. "Nobody else needs to know."

"Yeah, I can call him," Malu said, and sat up suddenly. "Dad, can you get my cellphone?"

Tracy looked at me. "Just for this one call," he said. "Then back in the drawer it goes."

"Dad ..." Malu whined.

"Just this one call," Tracy said again, and got up and left the room.

He returned a couple of moments later and Malu made the call.

CHAPTER ELEVEN

We met at a Burger King in the Kapa'a Shopping Center. I don't know why, but I was shocked to find a Burger King on the island. It just didn't seem to fit. It was like finding an empty plastic milk bottle in the folds of a pristine jungle.

I ordered a large Diet Coke and a Spam Crois-san'wich, then took my tray into what the Burger King folk referred to as a "dining room." It looked pretty much like every other Burger King I'd ever been to but with a dash here and there of island décor. I picked a table in the middle and sat down, taking a sip of my Diet Coke. It was pretty good but, then, it'd better be. It was nearly a buck more than what I paid in California.

As I unwrapped my Croissan'wich I scanned the room around me. There was a young man and a woman sitting at a table near the window, another woman with three bouncing kids taking up a booth in the corner, and an old man reading a newspaper, his coffee cup oozing steam into the atmosphere, minding his own business, the scowl on his face telling the world he wanted to keep it that way.

The first bite of the Croissan'wich dispelled any disappointment that there was a Burger King in paradise. With the addition of Spam the wonder meat, the Croissan'wich took on a new level of deliciousness. I briefly considered moving to Hawaii just so I could consume Spam on a regular basis. (And then I remembered that Marina would have to move over with me, and she would no doubt put an end to my Spam consumption in record time.)

I glanced at my watch. It was almost 10:30am. They were just about to stop serving breakfast. I considered grabbing another Croissan'wich while there was still time, but the thought of Marina put that idea to a quick death. I sipped at my soda and waited for Hilo. We had agreed to meet at 10:30 so he wasn't exactly late yet.

At 10:40, the doors opened, and Hilo walked in. I recognized him immediately although I'd never seen him before in my life. Except for the fact that he was about forty pounds heavier than Malu, they could have been twins … or at least brothers. He had the same long, unkempt hair, wore basically the same shorts and shirt (Hilo's was an Iron Maiden "Fear of the Dark" shirt) and a pair of beat-up sandals that looked, from where I sat, like they were about ready to fall apart.

He peered around the dining room and finally in my direction. I nodded my head and gave a little wave. A moment later, he was at the table.

"Are you Mr. Heller?" Hilo asked.

"That's me," I said. "And you're Hilo."

"Yes, sir," Hilo said.

"Want something to eat?"

"You buying?" Hilo asked and gave a short little laugh.

"I am," I said. "I'd recommend the Spam Crois-san'wich, but I think they stopped serving breakfast."

"That's okay," Hilo said. "I'll take a Whopper."

"Fries and a drink?"

"Sure. Thanks."

I told him to take a seat and went to order his food. The cashier told me they'd bring it to the table when it was ready, gave me a little plastic tent with a 13 printed on it, and I went back and joined Hilo.

"Coming right up," I said. "So, how long have you and Malu been friends?"

"Since we were kids," Hilo said, and I fought back a smile. *Shit, man*, I thought, *You're still a kid.*

"Like grammar school?" I asked.

"Maybe even kindy-garden," Hilo said. "I've known him a long time."

"So, you've lived here your entire life?"

"Well, my parents moved here when I was three," he said. "My dad's a construction worker and, back then, there was all kinds of work here."

"What about your mother?"

"She works at Starbucks now," Hilo said. "But back then she was a stay-at-home mom."

An employee came by with a tray full of food and set it on the table.

"Ketchup?" she asked.

"Sure," Hilo said.

The employee unceremoniously dumped a handful of ketchup packets onto Hilo's tray, scooped up the plastic number tent, and was gone.

"Eat that," I said. "And then we'll talk some more. I'm going to make a phone call."

"Thanks," Hilo said.

I walked outside and dialed up Marina. It was almost two o'clock in California. She was probably just getting back to her office after a morning in the field.

She answered on the second ring. "Well, hello, world traveler."

"Well, hello, gorgeous."

"How's it going out there?"

"Just getting started," I said. "Sitting down with one of Malu's friends. He was there at the time of the robbery."

"What's he say?"

"Haven't got that far yet," I said. "Talked to Malu this morning, though, and I gotta say I tend to believe him."

"He could just be a really good liar."

"He could be," I agreed. "But I don't think so. He's really scared."

"That doesn't mean anything," Marina said. "He should be scared, whether he did it or not."

"That's true," I said. "Well, like I said, I'm just getting started here. I've got a long way to go."

"So, what's with this friend?"

"His name's Hilo," I told her. "And he's known Malu most of his life. I'm hoping to get his story of what happened in that restroom that afternoon, to compare it with what Malu told me."

"What if he's a really good liar, too?" Marina asked.

"Then I'm fucked," I said. "And it won't be the first time."

"Nor the last," Marina said, with a playfully lascivious tone.

"Marina!" I said in *faux* shock. "You're gonna make me fly back home this minute!"

"You wish," she said. "Be careful, honey."

"That's all I am," I told her. "Miss you."

"Love you."

"Me, too."

I closed the connection and went back inside the Burger King, half expecting to see that Hilo had finished his meal and vacated the premises. But he was still there, poking the last of his fries into his mouth. I re-joined him at the table.

"So," I said. "My understanding is that Malu got involved with this group of malcontents only recently."

Hilo stared at me open-mouthed. Remnants of his last French fry were stuck between his front teeth.

"Malcontents," I said again. "Losers."

There was a word he understood, and I could tell he didn't like it. "You mean Sasha and her friends."

"Yes, tell me about Sasha," I said. "When did you first meet her?"

"It was only a couple of months ago," Hilo said. "Maybe four or five. Malu introduced me to her. She and her friends could get pot easy and Malu always had money to pay for it. They hung out all the time, smoking weed. I ran into them at the park one time, and they invited me over. Hung out with them after that."

"So, what happened after Malu stopped having money?"

"Sasha was *pissed*," Hilo said. "She started treating us like shit. Always putting pressure on Malu to get some money, even told him to steal it from his old man. But Malu wouldn't do that."

"So, whose idea was it to start robbing tourists?"

Hilo shook his head. "I don't know," he said. "It wasn't me or Malu, I know that for sure, but I don't think it was Sasha, either."

"How many people are in this group?" I asked.

"I dunno," Hilo said, scratching behind his right ear. "Seven or eight? Ten? I'm not sure." He laughed. "We just hang out together, man, we don't take inventory."

"No, I get it," I said. "I'm just trying to get a handle on this thing. So, somebody—we don't know who—decided it was a good idea to rob tourists to get pot money. Is that right so far?"

Hilo nodded.

"Okay, and then whose idea was it to start robbing tourists in the public restrooms?"

Hilo shook his head. "I don't remember that either," he said. "But it may have been *all* of ours. I remember sitting at a picnic table at some beach and we were all talking about it."

"How so?"

"It was like, how are we going to get money without getting caught? And then someone said the tourists always have money on them. And then someone else said how are we going to rob them if we don't have a gun. And I remember telling them, no guns. If there's guns, I'm out."

He rambled on for a while and I only half-listened. It didn't really matter whose idea any of this was. I just needed to find out what happened in that bathroom the night Matt Akana was murdered.

I let him go on for a couple of moments and jumped in when I found an opening.

"Okay, Hilo," I said. "Tell me about the night that guy got killed."

Hilo's eyes instantly became wide and frightened. He wriggled around in his seat nervously. "Man, I'm telling you, Malu and I had nothing to do with that."

"You didn't rob him?"

"No, we robbed him," Hilo admitted quickly, as though confessing to the lesser crime would clear him of the bigger one. "But he was alive when we left, I swear to God."

"Tell me everything, from the moment you went into the bathroom to the moment you were a mile away."

"It was the usual gig, man," Hilo said. "It was our turn, Malu and me."

"You took turns?"

"Yeah," Hilo said. "We decided it wasn't fair for one person to take all the risk, so we took turns. Me and Malu once, then Devin and Nathan next then Makala and Eddie."

"But never Sasha?"

"It was the *boys'* bathroom, man," Hilo said, and he seemed shocked that I'd even ask such a question.

"Of course," I said. "Now tell me about that day."

"We all drove down to Lydgate Beach because there's almost always tourists there. Sasha and the rest of them stayed in the van…"

"Your van."

Hilo nodded. "My van. And then Malu and I went into the bathroom. We waited, I don't know, for like forty-five minutes or so before we were ready."

"What do you mean by that?"

"Well, you couldn't just rob the first man who came in to take a leak," he said. "You know, some of them would come in with their kids, or there'd be someone taking a dump in one of the stalls. You had to time it just right, to make sure the guy was alone and that there was no one else around. Sometimes, we were in there for a while."

"And what were you doing while you were in there waiting?"

"Smoking," Hilo said. "Talking."

"Just standing in a public restroom for almost an hour, smoking and talking, and nobody ever thought that was suspicious?"

Hilo shrugged.

"Okay," I said. "So, this guy finally comes in, this Matt Akana ..."

"Was that his name?"

"Yeah," I said flatly. "That was his name. So, this guy finally comes in, he's alone, and there's no one but the two of you in the bathroom, smoking and talking."

"Yeah," Hilo said. "And so, we waited until he started pissing and then Malu went for his wallet, and I pulled down his pants."

"How'd he react?" I asked.

"Like they all do," Hilo said. "He was freaked out at first, and then just pissed. Malu got his wallet, and we were out the door. That guy tried to chase us, but his feet were all tangled up in his pants. I mean, it's hard to run when your pants are around your ankles."

He gave a little laugh.

"This shit isn't funny," I said. "There's a man who is dead now and you two were maybe the last ones to see him alive. Whether you guys had anything to do with his death or not isn't even important because your friend might go to jail for the rest of his life for it either way."

"Shit, man, don't get all serious …" Hilo started.

"No, we need to get serious, Hilo," I said. "Your little robberies weren't cute, they weren't funny, they were fucked up. You took advantage of innocent people when they were at their most vulnerable. And for what? So, you could smoke a fucking joint? So don't sit here and smirk at me and tell me what a great time you and your asshole friends had because, I swear to God, if you don't get serious about this, I am going to fuck up your life so badly that you'll wish you'd never met Malu Vang."

Hilo stared hard at me, and, for a moment, I thought I saw tears well up in his eyes. Then, he put he hands flat on the table and started to stand.

"Sit back down," I told him, in a tone that made it clear I wasn't kidding. "We're not done here yet."

Hilo sat.

"Now here's the next question, Hilo," I said. "Why haven't you gone to the police with your story?"

"They're looking for me," he said.

"No shit they're looking for you," I said. "And you've been hiding from them. You're the only person that can corroborate Malu's story and you're hiding like a god-damn coward. Why?"

"It's not that easy, man,' Hilo said.

"It *is* that easy," I told him. "Your friend is about to get life in prison for a murder you say he didn't commit. Yeah, it might cost you a few months of your life fessing up to the robberies, but does that really balance with Malu spending the rest of his life behind bars?"

"You don't understand," Hilo said quietly.

"Your damn right, I don't."

"I can't go to the police. I can't let them find me."

"Why? What are you hiding?"

"It's my parents, man," Hilo said. "If I go to the police, they'll be in trouble."

"What are you talking about?"

"My parents," Hilo said. "They're here illegally."

I blinked. "What are you talking about?" I said again.

"They're illegal aliens."

That was a phrase I was not expecting. "You mean they're … undocumented?"

"They're here illegally," Hilo said again. "I told you my dad came here for work when I was three years old, right? Well, my parents are from Mexico. They came over here to get jobs and, well, never got around to getting their citizenship."

"So, your real name isn't Hilo," I said.

"No," he said. "It's Mario. Mario Sanchez."

I shook my head in wonder.

"Did your parents have work visas?"

"I don't think they had anything," Hilo said. "They heard that there was plenty of work over here, they packed up the family, and they went to where the work was. Been working ever since."

"And you think that if the police find out, they'll be deported."

"They will be!" Hilo said. "The people they came over with all those years ago were just deported last month. Big ICE sweep."

"Well, I got news for you, mister," I said. "If the police go to your parents' house looking for you, odds are they're gonna do a little research on your parents, too. The only way to avoid this would have been not to get involved with the robberies in the first place."

"I know," Hilo said. "I feel like shit."

"You should," I told him. "You've put your family in a bad place, and you've put your friend in a bad place."

I saw the tears welling up in his eyes again.

"Listen, Hilo, let me talk to the police here. Maybe they can cut you a deal, maybe there's a way to fix this. But you can't leave Malu hanging. You can't let him take the heat for something he didn't do."

He sat across from me, staring down at the crumpled Whopper wrapper and empty fries carton on his tray. I could almost hear his mind working, going through the various scenarios, possibilities, and outcomes. I gave him the time he needed. I let him think.

After a couple of minutes, he looked up at me and his eyes were filled with a combination of frustration and fear. "No, man, I can't do it," he said. He backhanded the tray off the table, and it clattered to the ground loudly. Everyone else in the restaurant turned and looked our way.

And Hilo stood up, ran out of the dining room, and disappeared from sight.

I let him run. If there was another way to prove Malu wasn't a murderer, I'd find it. I had time. But now I had an ace up my sleeve. It wouldn't be hard to find Hilo again if I had to. The last thing I wanted to do was see his parents deported but, if I had to play that card to keep Malu out of prison, I'd play it.

But, as I had told Marina just a few minutes ago, I was just getting started.

CHAPTER TWELVE

I had asked Tracy for a car and he had given me one. It had to look local, and it had to be subtle, and it had to fit in. A Town Car or limo would stand out like a sore thumb, especially with the mountain of a man named Alika behind the wheel. A rental car would scream tourist. So, Tracy had provided me with the perfect vehicle: a 1989 Suzuki Samurai.

It was clunky and old and not in the best state of repair, but it was just what I needed, and it would get me from Point A to Point B which, on Kauai, were never too far apart. Tracy said he had planned on restoring it but just hadn't gotten around to it yet. I was glad. I could tool around in the Samurai all day and not get a second glance. That was all I really needed.

I was sitting behind the wheel in the Burger King parking lot and Googling on my phone. The search words "Matt Akana real estate" brought up an address in Princeville, back near where I was staying. There was nothing else to do at the moment, so I turned the key, started the Samurai, and headed North.

According to Tracy, the highest speed limit anywhere on Kauai was 50mph, and as I cruised through Kapa'a, I realized just how right he was. Traffic moved along at a bustling 25mph through town, moving up to 40mph as you came out on the other side. I guessed it would take me half an hour to make the twenty-mile drive.

Almost exactly thirty minutes later, I pulled into a parking lot that led to a tumble of restaurants and shops set up strip mall style and parked the Samurai near an ice cream shop. Ice cream sounded pretty good right now. There was no air conditioning in the Samurai and the temperature was inching toward 90. A cool double dip cone would go down wonderfully. I resisted, mainly because I'd just had a delicious Spam Croissan-wich but also because I had other things to do beside eat ice cream.

I wandered around the shops for a while, peeking in the windows of a few gift shops, passing through a busy supermarket, and visiting the food court which contained a Chinese place, a Mexican take-out and a Tiki Bar that looked like a lot of fun. I made a note to come back here later.

Eventually, I stumbled upon a directory near a HELICOPTER RIDES kiosk and read carefully through the listing. There it was, in the M's, of course: MATTHEW AKANA REAL ESTATE KAUAI. The office was on the second floor of Building C. I found the YOU ARE HERE icon on the directory and navigated with my finger from that point to Building C. Easy Peasy.

A few minutes later, I found the building I was looking for. There were no shops in this particular building but instead there were several business offices and a dentist. I took a circular walk along the elevated boardwalk, pretending to look at everything. As I came round to the staircase a second time, I walked calmly and confidently up the stairway.

It wasn't that I thought anybody might be watching me, but I was unclear as to whether the real estate office had been marked as a crime scene. Or, if Matt Akana had a partner who might be working. Better safe than sorry.

Akana's office was two doors down from the stairs. It was your typical real estate office, complete with photos of available properties taped to the windows. I glanced through them briefly. There were time shares available for anywhere from $11,000 to $60,000. There were beach front properties going for $3.8 million to $12 million. And there was one estate available whose current owner was asking $38 million.

All were above my pay grade.

After what I considered a convincing moment that I was here to maybe buy some land I tried the doorknob. Locked, of course, but it appeared to be a standard Kwikset doorknob that I knew I could easily pick. I glanced over my shoulder to see if the coast were clear.

It wasn't. A woman stood on the landing in what I assumed was Building B, watching me. I gave her a quick wave, shrugged, and walked away from the door. She returned the favor with a quick wave of her own and then went back to smoking her cigarette. Now was obviously not the time to break and enter.

Tracy had made dinner reservations for us at the St. Regis hotel at 6pm which meant I still had plenty of time to explore. I decided to start my exploration at the Tiki Bar I'd passed earlier. I walked down the stairway and headed in that direction.

The bar was called the Tiki Iniki, and I fell in love with the place the moment I walked in. It looked like the kind of bar you'd find on Gilligan's Island, with bamboo décor everywhere and barstools whose bases looked like Tiki statues. Glass globes in fish nets hung from the thatched ceiling and there was at least one puffer fish who'd been turned into a lamp, its face forever frozen in a surprised (and illuminated) expression. And the wall of booze bottles lining the back of the bar was promise of good things to come.

There were what looked like about ten stools sitting around the bar, all but three of them filled at the moment, so I took one of the available seats and grabbed the cocktail menu on the bar.

"Hey, what's up?" asked the gentleman to my left. He wore a pair of tan cargo shorts and a CALIFORNIA IS FOR LOVERS t-shirt. As a trained detective, I knew that meant he was probably a tourist. A tourist who was currently feeling no pain.

"Doing better now," I told him. "I found a bar."

"Got that right," he laughed.

"What are you drinking there?" I asked him.

"Mai Tai!" he said proudly, holding up the turquoise ceramic mug in the shape of a tiki carving. "They make the best ones here."

I nodded, thinking that every single bar on the island probably makes that claim. But a Mai Tai sounded good.

"Sold!" I said, and when the bartender came over a moment later, I ordered one up.

As I waited for my libation to be served, I thought about what I'd learned today, which wasn't much. Malu had told me his story, and I was inclined to believe it. It wasn't so much his convincing performance, but the fact that they had committed thirteen of these robberies and that none of them had involved violence. Why, suddenly, bring a rock along from outside and brain your victim instead of just yanking his pants down? Something about that didn't click.

Then there was my conversation with Hilo, aka Mario. I was just as inclined to believe him. His story and Malu's story matched for virtually every detail. As for his unwillingness to go to the police, it seemed impossible to me that he had the smarts to make that story up. I wondered if it even really mattered. I wasn't sure how great a witness he'd be, considering his marijuana use and the fact he was part of a robbery ring.

The thing about his parents disturbed me. I'd never even considered the possibility of illegal aliens in Hawaii. It seemed far-fetched, although of course it was plausible. It was something you'd expect in states like California, Arizona, and Texas, but Hawaii? I picked up my iPhone and hit the Google app. A moment later, I entered the search words "Kauai, illegal aliens" and then ENTER. When the results popped up, the fourth headline down told me all I needed to know: ILLEGAL ALIENS ARRESTED ON KAUAI. I clicked the link and read the article there. Apparently, "ten Mexicans, one El Salvadoran and one Guatemalan" had been arrested for "working illegally for an off-Island contractor" and had been deported by Homeland Security. So, the problem of illegal aliens in Kauai was obviously quite real.

My Mai Tai arrived, and I toasted my new friend at the bar. He slapped my shoulder and told me to "Drink up!" I took his advice. The Mai Tai was good, not the cherry red concoction you get in California at places like Red Robin but closer to the original recipe created by Trader Vic. It was spiced and cold and delicious, and I could taste the rum. So good I decided I may have another.

Two Mai Tais later, I headed back out to the Samurai and drove home to The Cliffs. I changed from shorts and sandals into my Pink Floyd swim trunks, grabbed a towel and headed out to the pool. Hell, I was in paradise. I might as well enjoy a little of it while I was here.

I hadn't been in the sun for more than ten minutes when my phone rang. It was Jay Huihui.

"Can you meet?"

"Now?"

"Yeah."

"Where?"

"Lei Petite."

"What?"

"Lei Petite. Coffee and pastry shop in the Princeville Center."

"I was just over there," I said.

"So, can we meet?"

"Now?"

"Now," Jay said. And I could hear his impatience starting to surface.

"Ten minutes," I said.

"Close enough."

CHAPTER THIRTEEN

Even though he was the one who had called the meeting, I made it to Lei Petite before Jay arrived. It was just about closing time, but I was able to get my hands on a mango scone and an iced green tea before they shooed me out and closed the door behind me. I sat on the nearby patio, ate my scone and drank my tea, and felt the heat squeeze the perspiration right out of me.

Ten minutes later, Jay arrived. He plopped down un-apologetically in the seat beside me and slid over a large bubble-lined Kraft envelope. I picked it up and took a peek. Inside was a Taurus 905 9mm revolver and a couple of boxes of ammo. I sealed the envelope with its built-in clasp and left it on the table.

"Thanks," I said. "Is it clean?"

Jay nodded. "Unregistered."

"Thanks," I said again.

"Just so you know, this wasn't my idea," Jay said.

"I understand."

"Good," Jay said. "Then let's lay down some ground rules. First, despite the fact I gave this to you ... or maybe *because* I gave this to you ... don't be shooting anybody. I won't be filling out a shitload of paperwork if you use this because I'll be *fired on the spot*. Paperwork will be the last of my problems. Savvy?"

"Savvy," I said. "But what if someone else shoots at me first?"

Jay ignored me. "Second," he said. "If you get some kind of lead on this, whether it implicates Malu or not, you come to me first, understand? Tracy and I have been friends a long time, but this is business. If the kid did this, then he's going to pay the price for it."

"I don't think he did it."

"I don't want to think he did it," Jay said. "But if he did, he's going down. Agreed?"

"Agreed."

"Third, treat this place like it's your own hometown. Don't make a mess here. I don't need you unearthing things that don't need unearthing. You come across something funky, you come to me. If I can't figure out, I'll move it up the food chain. But we want to keep this thing on the down low. The last thing I need is for brass to find out I was aiding and abetting an out of state detective in investigating a crime that took place on our turf. Savvy?"

"Savvy," I said. "Do you watch a lot of police movies? Because you talk that way. You know with the 'up the food chains' and the 'turfs' and the 'savvys'? I'm just curious."

"Don't be a smart ass," Jay said. "I'm serious."

"So am I," I said. "And I don't need to be told how to behave. This isn't my first rodeo."

Jay smiled humorlessly. "I see somebody else has been watching police movies, too."

"Where else you going to learn all the lingo?"

Tracy pushed the Kraft envelope back toward me and stood. "Like I said, don't be shooting anybody. And call me if you come up with anything."

"Righty-O."

Jay walked briskly away. I watched him until he disappeared around a corner, then I scooped up the gun, tucked it under my arm and headed back to the Samurai.

Chapter Fourteen

The St. Regis Hotel in Kauai is lush by anyone's standards, and by "anyone" I'm including the likes of Bill Gates, Jeff Bezos, or Julius Caesar.

It is sprawled on a cliff on the Northern side of Kauai, and its unique vantage point makes it one of the best places on the island to catch the legendary sunsets there. In fact, people from all over the world journey to the bar there, where the enormous, wall-sized windows make for perfect viewing and picture-taking as the sun drops into the West. If there are such a thing as five-star hotels, then

St. Regis should probably be a six-star hotel, maybe even seven, and, once again, is far above my pay grade.

But not Tracy Vang's.

Alika had picked me up at my room promptly at 5:45 and maneuvered the Lincoln up to Ka Haku Road. From there it was just a few short minutes to the St. Regis. He dropped me off near the valet desk and told me that Tracy was waiting for me inside at the Kauai Grill. I walked inside and felt dwarfed and humbled by the magnificent surroundings. The glory of the St. Regis felt fit for kings.

I wandered through the lobby in awe, my eyes wide with wonder at the stunning architecture and décor. I wondered what it must feel like to afford this type of splendor and whether its majesty ever wore off or became mundane. I couldn't imagine how.

"Kauai Grill?" I asked a passing employee. She stopped and, with a smile that brightened the area around her, pointed to my left. I thanked her and marched on.

The gentleman at the podium offered me another effusive smile as I approached. He wore a pair of long shorts and a nice button up tan shirt with a pink hibiscus print. I preferred his attire tenfold to that of the stuffy maître d's I'd encountered elsewhere.

"I have a dinner reservation," I said. "With Tracy Vang. I believe he's already arrived?"

"Mr. Vang, yes, sir," the man told me. "Right this way, sir."

And he led me into the Kauai Grill.

It was almost like walking onto the bridge of a starship. Not that there were consoles with flashing lights surrounding me and not that it had a high tech feel but rather that the room was dominated by its ceiling, which was illuminated with a mammoth circular lighting system, broken into irregular quadrilaterals. At its center was a solid circle from which a massive chandelier hung, a few dozen strands of what looked like crystal jellyfish tentacles dangling beneath.

"Brace! Over here!" I heard Tracy call. I glanced around and found him at a booth near the window, which spanned the entire wall in front of me. Beyond the window was a view of the bay, with the sun glowing a soft fuzzy yellow above the silhouette of magnificent Mount

Makana. No postcard in the world could have done justice to its jaw-dropping beauty.

Tracy was sprawled out comfortably in his seat, wearing a pair of tan board shorts, a flowery Vang t-shirt, and a pair of those neon plastic sunglasses that almost perfectly matched his shirt. I walked over and took the seat beside him. There was a bottle of Makers Mark and two highball glasses on the table in front of us. "I took the liberty of ordering the first round," Tracy said, handing me one of the glasses. "I assume you drink it neat."

"I do," I said accepting the glass and taking a sip.

"Do you prefer the 46 or the original?" Tracy asked me, settling back into the plush leather seat. "I like them both," he went on. "But the 46 seems a little more ... I don't know, *harsh*, I guess."

"I'm with you, Trace," I said. "I'll take the original over the 46, but my favorite is the Cask Strength."

"Dammit, I should've ordered that," Tracy said, sitting up and searching for a server.

"No, no, no," I said. "This is perfect." I drank a little more, just to show Tracy I was serious. "Tracy, I got to tell ya, this place is beautiful, man. I've never been any-where like this."

Tracy grinned. "Wait until the sun sets," he said. "It's awesome."

The server came by and left us with some menus. They were exquisitely printed on heavy paper and proba-bly cost five bucks each to produce. We drank our bour-bon and chatted. Tracy told me that the hotel used to be the Princeville Hotel but was re-opened in 2009 as the St. Regis. He told me that the site of the hotel was known as Pu'u Pa'oa, which broke down to "mountain" and "staff of the Fire Goddess."

"You mean, staff, like … office assistants and such?"

Tracy laughed. "No, staff like a walking stick, but that of a Goddess. Pele, who was the Fire Goddess, would strike her staff into the earth when she was searching for a new home, creating huge craters. Down below the hotel is Kamo'omaika'i, what's left of an ancient fishpond that was built way back in prehistoric times."

"One of Pele's craters?"

"So, they say," said Tracy.

"This place is just full of history and lore, isn't it?"

"It sure is," Tracy said, clinking his glass against mine and re-filling both.

A server came to take our dinner order and Tracy didn't hesitate. "We're celebrating," he told her. "I haven't seen this man in nearly twenty years. So, I'm going big. I'll have the lobster."

"The grilled whole kona lobster," said the server, committing it to memory. "And you, sir?"

"I'm going to do both coasts," I said. "Surf & Turf."

"Half Kona Lobster and six-ounce beef tenderloin. Very good." She glanced at our bottle of Maker's Mark, now more than half empty. "Something else to drink?"

"Water would be good," I said.

"*Very* good," said Tracy, and laughed.

"So, tell me, Tracy, how's business?" I asked, as our server sauntered away.

Tracy beamed that famous smile. "Business is *great*," he said. "We're growing on every level. Board sales are up, clothing sales are through the roof. We just opened our first store in Belgium. *Belgium*. Not exactly the first country you think of when you think surf wear."

"That's for sure," I said. "Is there even a *beach* there?"

"Actually, there is," Tracy laughed. "In the North Sea. Not exactly the world's best surfing but it is what it is."

The sun dipped a little more behind Mount Makana and I heard a group of people at the bar across the way coo with delight. I glanced over and saw a man standing over a bottle of champagne, wielding a sword of some type.

"What the hell is that?" I asked. "Some kind of samurai thing?"

Tracy laughed again. "No, it's the Saber Ritual," he said. "Well, the *champagne* ritual, actually. They make a toast to the sunset, then that dude uses the saber to remove the cork. They share the champagne with people who have special events—birthdays, anniversaries, and the like—and together they watch the sun set."

"They sure make a big deal about the sunset over here," I said.

"And in just a few minutes," Tracy said. "You'll see why."

As if on cue, the sun dipped down behind Mt. Makana and the world went bright with color. Oranges and reds lit up the sky, and the entire horizon seemed to burn with a ribbon of fire. As we watched, enraptured, the view darkened quickly and then, with a final pop of light, the sun was gone.

There was a round of applause from the guests of the St. Regis.

"Very nice," I said, but secretly was thinking that the sunsets in Ventura were just as beautiful.

"So, Brace, tell me about your day," Tracy said.

I pushed back into the booth, leaned against the cushion there, and sipped at my Makers Mark. "Well, I learned a few things today," I said.

"Such as?"

"First, and perhaps most important, I believe Malu. I don't think he killed that man."

I could see a wave of relief wash over Tracy's features.

"That doesn't give him a pass," I continued. "The fact of the matter is that he put himself in that position, and he's got to pay the piper for the robbery."

"Absolutely," Tracy said. "And he knows that, too. We've talked about it at length."

"But he shouldn't have to pay for something he didn't do," I said. "I spoke with his friend, Hilo, today, and his story jibes with Malu's. He confirmed that when they left that rest room Matt Akana was still alive."

Tracy pounded his fist on the table. "Well, there it is!" he said. "Let's get him to talk with the police, tell them that Malu didn't do it!"

"It's not that easy," I said. "Hilo won't talk to the police."

Tracy looked as though someone had slapped him. "Why the hell not?" he spat.

"He has his reasons," I said.

"What the hell are you talking about, Brace? What reasons? What possible reasons could he have that are more important than my son going to jail?"

"Malu isn't going to jail, at least for murder," I said. "And if I have to pressure Hilo, I'll do it. But, Tracy, I'm just getting started on this. I mean, I've been on this case just about eight hours. Give me some time. And trust me."

Tracy fell back into the chair, like a marionette whose strings had just been cut. He gulped down the last of the Makers Mark in his highball and looked up at me over the top of his silly glasses. "I do trust you, Brace. You know I do. But he's my son. My only son."

"A fact I am well aware of," I said. "And I'm going to protect him."

"So, what's next?"

"I don't know exactly," I said, which was the wrong thing to say because Tracy gave me an ugly glance. "Listen, this is how these things work. I'm going to stick my nose into everything, I'm going to look under every rock, in every cranny. Something will turn up, it always does. And we'll clear Malu of the murder charge, I promise."

Tracy shook his head. "How can you promise?"

"Because that's what you're paying me to do," I said. "And I am one tenacious son of a bitch."

That got a smile out of Tracy. "If there's anything I remember about you in high school," Tracy said. "It was that." He grinned again. "That and the fact you wrote poetry."

"It wasn't poetry," I said. "They were dirty limericks. There's a difference."

"I actually remember one," Tracy said. "*There once was a shark in the sea; who found it quite painful to pee …*"

And then, thankfully, the server showed up with our dinners and the rest of my infamous high school poetry faded from Tracy's lips, hopefully never to be resurrected again.

CHAPTER FIFTEEN

Tracy and I enjoyed our dinner and conversation and then called it a night. He suggested a night cap at the St. Regis bar, but I politely declined and reminded him that we'd just finished a bottle of Makers Mark together.

But the real story was that it was already 10:30 and I still had work to do.

Alika was waiting outside with the Lincoln and drove me back to The Cliffs through the dark streets. He insisted on escorting me back to my room, but I told him that wasn't necessary. "I'm a big boy," I told him. "I can find my way back all by myself."

Alika didn't seem convinced but allowed me to give it a try.

Once inside, I quickly changed into a pair of black jeans and a solid black t-shirt, slipped into my flip-flops, and tucked my card key into my back pocket. My lock pick bag went into the front. I waited quietly for about half an hour for the world outside to settle and then headed back out the door.

Earlier I had calculated that Matt Akana Real Estate was less than two miles away from my room and that I could walk that distance easily in twenty-five to thirty minutes. The sky was heavy with the threat of rain, and I hoped that it would hold out for at least another couple of hours so I could get to Akana's office, do what I needed to do and get back before it started to pour. Based on the humidity and the temperature surrounding me, I felt that the odds of that were slim.

The stars and moon were virtually my only light as I wound my way through the various resorts and came once again to Ka Haku Road. There, I found an asphalt pedestrian path that ran parallel to both the road and the

Makai Golf Course, and I followed that in the dark until I reached a grassy public park. In the distance, I could hear the happy sounds of partiers at the Tiki Iniki bar and suddenly wished I had brought along my wallet. Then again, a guy in all black with only a card key and a bag of lock picks might draw some unwanted attention sitting on a barstool in Kauai.

I came around the back of the strip mall and made my way to Building C. I stopped for a moment, pretending to warm my hands, and then realized how stupid that was considering how close I was to the equator. I glanced around, confirmed the coast was clear, and quietly walked up the stairway to the second floor.

Matt Akana's Real Estate was exactly the way I'd left it. As far as I could tell, no one had been in or out of the place since this afternoon. I glanced over my shoulder. My friend with the cigarette was nowhere to be seen. I dropped to my knees and, using the tiny flashlight in my lock pick bag, went to work.

This particular Kwikset knob wasn't meant for heavy duty protection, and I had it unlocked in mere moments.

I opened the door, thankful that its hinges didn't squeak, stepped inside, and closed it behind me.

My first thought was that Akana apparently had no partner after all. There were seven or eight client chairs sitting around the office and only one desk. On the desk was a wood-grain name plate engraved, in bright white letters, MATT AKANA. Below that, in small cursive letters, *Your Guide to Living in Paradise!*

Like any other real estate office on the planet, this one was wall-papered with photos of houses and properties. I gave them only a cursory glance and then took a seat behind the desk. I fumbled for the power button on the desktop computer there and, when my fingertips found it, gave it was quick push. As the computer hummed to life, I went through the drawers on either side of me. Nothing very interesting there, save for a pink, fist-sized squeeze ball with the image of a brown nipple and the phrase HELP US SUPPORT BREAST HEALTH stamped on it. Probably more of a novelty joke item than promotional schwag, I thought.

The computer monitor flashed a WINDOWS 10 logo and then dissolved into a sunny beach photo. I was thankful no PLEASE ENTER PASSWORD warning flashed there. I gripped the mouse on the pad beside the keyboard and did a little clicking.

Half an hour later, I turned off the computer and punched the off button on the monitor. If there was anything useful in there, I had either missed it or misunderstood it. Either way, the computer was all but useless.

I turned my attention to the two in-boxes on the desktop. The first, on the left, had two manila folders in it, one labeled "Receipts" and the other "Mileage." As my impressive detective skills predicted, the "Receipts" file was full of receipts for lunches and dinners that Akana must have treated clients to. And the "Mileage" folder was just that—a history of where he had driven and why.

In the second in-box, on the right, was a stack of more substantial folders. They were blue, their sides made of pressboard card stock, and the insides were pierced with Acco prong fasteners. They had addresses printed in ballpoint on their tabs, with listings in places such as Kapa'a, Hanalei, and Princeville. Each folder was packed with photos of different properties, both interiors and exteriors, and a fact sheet with information about the number of bathrooms and bedrooms and square footage of each.

The folder on the bottom, however, was different than the others. It was blue as well, and solid, like the rest, but inside was only one sheet of paper. It was completely blank except for one number, printed in the middle: $14,000,000. But the first two numbers had been crossed out with a red marker and reversed so it now read $41,000,000. I flipped the folder on its side and read the tab there. HANAKAPI'AI BEACH PROJECT it said.

Otherwise, the folder was empty.

Hmmm, I thought. Could this be a clue?

I cursed myself for not bringing my phone. If I had, all it would take was a few fast shutter-clicks and I'd be out of here. Then I realized that Mr. Akana wasn't going to be missing that folder any time soon and tucked the entire thing beneath my arm.

I heard the creak of the wooden boardwalk and froze as someone walked past the front door. A moment later, I relaxed as the sound of their feet headed down the stairs. Probably just someone who'd had too many Mai Tais looking for the restroom. With my prize tucked safely beneath my arm, I approached the front door, listened closely a moment, and then opened and closed it behind me, clicking the lock button and making sure it closed securely.

I headed back to my room with a new bounce to my step. I had something, a mystery to explore that might lead to something else. Tracy had looked a little wary when I told him I didn't know what my next step was.

I really wish he could have seen me now.

CHAPTER SIXTEEN

In the gloom of the rainy new morning, my midnight discovery was starting to look a little less world changing than I originally hoped.

I was sitting on the balcony of my room at The Cliffs, eating a bag of Hostess Chocolate Donuts and drinking a Coke Zero. It was raining hard. Water ran off the rooftop in rivers and fat drops splatted to their deaths on the edges of the balcony near where I was sitting.

Not balcony. *Lanai.* I was in Hawaii, after all.

It was more than just a shower; it was a downpour. I could barely see the ocean from where I sat, and it was only a few hundred feet away.

I took another sip of Coke Zero and then picked up my blue folder. I opened it and closed it, turned it to and fro, even shook it a little to see if something would fall out. Of course, nothing did. I held it horizontally and let the light bounce off it, hoping I would catch the impressions of a note there, something someone had written on another piece of paper and the pencil or pen tip had pushed through to the cardboard surface of the folder. Just like you see in the movies. But there was nothing. All I had was just a blue folder with a single piece of paper in it. A single piece of paper on which was printed a single, eight-digit number.

Not just a number, but a dollar amount: $41,000,000. That was a lot of Simoleons, even to someone like Tracy Vang.

I closed the folder and examined the tab. There was a plain, self-adhesive label stuck there with the words HANAKAPI'AI BEACH PROJECT hand-written on it.

I snatched up my phone and Googled HANAKAPI'AI BEACH. The first headline to pop up was a story on TripAdvisor.com asking people not to swim at this beach due to "rough water" and "huge waves." I clicked on the link and discovered that the only way to get to Hanaka-pi'ai Beach was to follow a "strenuous and muddy" walking path that stretched nearly four miles. Sounded like a walk I wasn't interested in taking.

I clicked on the IMAGES tag and the screen changed from words to photos, one of which was a hand-carved sign warning of "unseen currents" that "have killed" (according to the tally marks that followed) more than seventy people. The waters were so rough there that at least fifteen drowning victims had never been found.

Most of the images, however, were maps of Kauai. I chose one of the larger ones and then pinched the screen to zoom in on Hanakapi'ai Beach. It was located on the Northwest side of the island, not too far from Princeville, and I figured I could probably drive there in half an hour or so, even with the rain.

I glanced at my watch. It was 10am. The rain showed no sign of easing up. *Screw it*, I thought. *I'm going to the beach.*

I ate another chocolate donut, drank the rest of my Coke Zero and padded upstairs where I slipped into a pair of jeans, an AC/DC t-shirt, and the pair of old sneakers I always brought along just in case Tevas weren't acceptable. I dropped my phone into my front pocket, slid the gun into the back of my pants, and headed downstairs.

The one thing I hadn't considered about the Samurai was whether or not it was watertight. As I slid into the driver's seat and felt the cold moisture seeping immediately onto my buttocks, I realized that maybe I should have thought of that. It was too late now, I was already wet, so I started up the car and headed out.

I drove up to the Kuhio highway and turned right. As the Samurai accelerated so did the rain seeping through the gasket at the windshield. There was more water spraying into my face than falling from the sky. I slipped on the pair of purple Vang sunglasses that Tracy had given me and was grateful that they kept most of the water out of my eyes.

I followed a hairpin turn and began a slow descent down toward the village of Hanalei. There was a tiny, one-lane, steel bridge there spanning the Hanalei River, and I had to stop on my side and wait while a convoy of four cars crossed from the other. When the last car passed me, I hurried over the bridge and headed toward Hanalei.

Hanalei Bridge. Hanalei River. Village of Hanalei. Somebody hadn't been very creative when it came to naming landmarks in this area.

I drove through Hanalei at the typical 25mph speed limit and caught sight of what looked like a delightful bar, the Tahiti Nui. Now I had a place to stop on my way back, assuming I didn't drown in the Samurai on the way. The odds were against me. Leaving the village behind, I drove through a series of what looked like floating bridges, one lane each, and small thin roads that followed the coastline closely, undulating like a moving snake. There were homes out this way and they were glorious. Many sat above ground, on poles, which I assumed was to prevent flooding in the wetter months.

I passed a sign reading TUNNELS BEACH and the name seemed to leap out at me. Then I remembered the surfer whose arm had been bitten off by a tiger shark there, and her heroic story that had become what they love to call a "major motion picture."

Finally, I came to the end of the road. Literally. I was at a place called Ke'e Beach and the road simply ended, turning into a parking lot instead. There were only a few cars here, but the lot was probably at least half full. The rain, heavy as it was, hadn't kept everyone away. I parked in a spot near the entrance, set the brake and turned off the engine.

I dug my cellphone out of my pocket and was unsurprised to see the NO SERVICE label staring back at me. I was at the end of the road, after all.

Well, not exactly. I waited until the rain seemed to ease just a little and stepped out of the car. I walked past the other parking places to the very end of the Kuhio Highway. It just stopped suddenly, ending in a roundabout that gave you just enough room to turn around and head back.

But there was a dirt pathway there, leading off into the jungle, and a sign that read: "Kalalau: This is sacred land. Give it your utmost care, respect and leave knowing you have preserved it for future generations."

I stared hard at that pathway for a few moments, wavering between taking the path now and seeing where it went, waiting until later when perhaps it was drier, or going back to the resort and Googling photos that other, braver souls had taken.

It was then that the rain picked up again, hammering rain drops that felt the size of fists into my shoulders and back, and I decided to hoof it back to the Samurai and see what delicious libations Tahiti Nui had to offer.

CHAPTER SEVENTEEN

I got back to the Cliffs with a couple of Mai Tais and most of a Hawaiian Pizza in my stomach and, as I toweled off the rain that hadn't already soaked irretrievably into my skin, I thought about several things. One, I still had no idea what my fancy blue folder meant. Two, I was no closer to proving Malu hadn't committed murder. And Three, I had heard that pineapple wasn't native to Hawaii so why was a ham and pineapple pizza called Hawaiian?

Once I was dry (enough), I slipped into my usual uniform (shorts, sandals, and the Tiki Iniki t-shirt I had purchased yesterday), poured myself a Makers Mark and went out to the lanai.

Whatever the blue folder from Matt Akana Real Estate was about, it had something to do with Hanakapi'ai Beach, or perhaps the surrounding area. My advanced sleuthing skills and the label on the folder helped guide me to that conclusion. I took my own earlier advice and spent some time Googling on my iPad, looking at photos that others had taken of the beach, the trail to get there, and the surrounding areas. It was all beautiful and green, that much was certain, but nothing there caught my eye as far as related to the folder or Malu.

After about twenty minutes, I shut down my browser and put the tablet face down on the table in front of me. I was tired of staring at the screen, and I had used Google so much in the past couple of days that I felt I should offer them part of my detective fee.

The problem was that I didn't know enough about Kauai to deduce what the Sam Hill was going on here. This was my first visit to "The Garden Isle" and all I knew about it was that my friend Tracy Vang lived here with his son, that it seemed to rain all the goddamned time, and that the Mai Tais were all pretty good … so far. What I needed to do was spend some time picking the brains of someone who knew Kauai better than I did. Somebody who'd spent more than two short days here.

A light bulb flashed in my brain as though paparazzi had been hiding there. I snatched my phone off the table and punched in a number. It rang on the other end a couple of times and then a voice answered, "Yes, Mr. Heller. How can I help you?"

"Hey, Alika," I said. "You got a couple of minutes? I'd like to pick your brain."

There was the briefest moment of silence and then Alika said, "I can be there in half an hour. Is that soon enough?"

"That's perfect. I'll make sure the beer's cold."

I ended the call and killed off the bourbon in my glass. Then I went back into the house, raided the refrigerator, and put together a rough but acceptable cheese plate.

After all, I was having a guest.

CHAPTER EIGHTEEN

Alika arrived at my front door in full chauffer regalia. "Dude," I said, as I beckoned him in. "This was more of a social call. You didn't have to dress to the nines for me."

"It was no trouble, sir," Alika said, stepping into the alcove and kicking off his shoes. "I appreciate the invitation."

I guided him to the lanai and through the sliding doors. His massive shoulders barely fit through the opening. "Please sit down," I told him and, as he did, I went back to the kitchen and retrieved the cheese plate I had made plus a pair of Maui Brewing Company cans labeled with the graphic of a blonde girl in a grass skirt and the moniker Bikini Blonde Lager.

I set the food and drinks on the table and took a seat opposite Alika. He nodded his thanks for the beer, popped it open with a mighty finger, and gave me a disappointed frown. "I am sorry for the rain, sir," he said. "When it is sunny here, it is warm and bright. When it rains, it is gray and gloomy."

"Not exactly your fault, Alika," I said, pulling the tab of my beer. "But I appreciate the sentiment." I took a sip of the lager and smiled. Not my favorite style of beer, but not bad.

We drank and ate crackers and cheese for a few moments, listening to the rain patter on the roof above and the lawn below us. I was surprised at how loud it really was, like drums in the jungle.

"So, you've worked for Tracy for eleven years," I said after a moment. "And how long have you lived in Kauai?"

"Born here," Alika said. "Near Koloa." He gave me a meek, sort of embarrassed look. "I've never actually left the island," he said.

"Really?" I asked, surprised. "But I thought you said you worked security for Tracy before you became his driver? You must have had to join him when he was overseas?"

Alika shook his head. "No. My job was to protect him here, at home." He smiled again. "I've never even been on a plane."

"Wow," I said. "I'm going to recommend Tracy give you a vacation somewhere. Like Tahiti. Or Las Vegas."

"No, sir, please don't," Alika said, and I was surprised at the depth of his embarrassment. "There is no need for you to do that, sir."

"Relax, Alika," I told him. "I was just half-kidding."

A wave of relief washed over him. I was touched by the man's unwavering loyalty, that he would be so embarrassed if someone spoke to his boss about him.

"Listen, Alika, I need to ask you a few questions about some places on the island," I said. "I'm just shooting in the dark here so feel free to tell me anything you know, okay? Like I said, this is more of a social occasion. I just want to get to know you a little better, and to know Kauai a little better."

Alika nodded. "I understand," he said. And took another sip of beer. The can looked tiny in his massive paw.

"What can you tell me about Hanakapi'ai Beach?" I asked, and the word was loose in my mouth like a fistful of BBs.

"Hanakapi'ai Beach," Alika said carefully, as though expecting me to repeat it. "It is a difficult beach to get to. You must follow The Kalalau Trail several miles to get there. The guides will tell you it's a 'moderate' hike, but it is really tougher than that. Many who try it either don't finish or have to be carried back. The beach is about two and a half miles in over wet terrain and many switchbacks. You must be fit to attempt it."

He gave me a look that said I probably wasn't fit enough to attempt it, but I let it pass because he was a new friend.

"Is it a State Beach?"

Alika screwed up his eyes. "I don't think it is a State Beach," he said. "But it may be part of the State Park there, the Napali Coast State Wilderness Park, I think it is called."

"Is there any private land out that way?"

Alika shook his head. "Not that I am aware of. But there is some controversy among the longtime residents in the area. Some of them believe that certain areas of the State Park actually belong to them, that they are sacred lands."

"Have there been any issues regarding that?" I asked. "Protests? Violence?"

"There have been protests," Alika said. "But they have been mild."

I absorbed this for a moment, then asked, "Can you think of any reason there would be a real estate deal going down out there? Any property out that way that might have been for sale?"

"To be the best of my knowledge, that would not be possible," Alika said. "That land is owned by the State of Hawaii or the Federal Government. It is not for sale."

"That's what I kind of figured," I said. "Another beer?"

"Yes, please," Alika said, crushing the can in his fist like a bug in a catcher's mitt. "What do you think of our local beer, Mr. Heller? Is it to your liking?"

"I like it just fine, Alika." I stepped into the kitchen, grabbed a couple more cold cans, and came back out to the lanai.

"I'd like to get a better look at that beach," I told Alika. "But I'm not looking forward to that hike, especially in this weather. Is there another way to get out there?"

"The trail is the only way," he said. "And boats are not permitted to land there."

"I'm not so worried about *landing*," I said. "I just want to get a look."

Alika thought for a moment. "I know a sea captain," he said. "A man with a fishing boat. He offers charters for fishermen. If you'd like, I can talk to him and see if he'd be willing to take you out for a look."

"That would be great, Alika."

"He will not land there," he said.

"I know," I told him. "I don't want him to. I just want to get close enough so I can check it out, maybe through a pair of binoculars."

"I will call him," Alika said. "And tell him you require his services."

"Thanks."

We sat, finished our beers, ate the rest of the cheese and crackers and then Alika said goodbye. He promised to get back to me in an hour or two and I thanked him and sent him on his way.

My phone rang. It was Marina. I took a quick look at the clock on the wall. It was 1:30 in the afternoon my time; 4:30 hers.

"Hi, honey," I said, after punching the accept button.

"Brace," Marina said sadly. "I miss you already."

We talked for half an hour, me filling her in on my case so far, she telling me about the elderly woman she'd spent the afternoon with, listening to tales of ages long gone. Our conversation only made us wish we were together sooner rather than later. We exchanged I Love Yous and disconnected.

Almost immediately, the phone rang again. Alika.

"You are all set up, Mr. Heller," he said. "Captain Newton will meet you at the Hanalei pier tomorrow at 7:30am."

"I'll be there."

And then I sat in the dark for a while, thinking about Tracy and Malu Vang, missing Marina and Wurzel, and turning the mystery of the $41,000,000 Hanakapi'ai Beach Project over and over in my mind.

CHAPTER NINETEEN

The sun decided to honor us with its presence the next morning and I was up and ready to go meet Captain Newton. I had every intention of driving the Samurai but was surprised to find Alika waiting downstairs with the Navigator.

"Well, good morning, Alika," I said. "Didn't expect to see you here today."

"And yet here I am," Alika said. "Good morning, sir."

He opened the back door and I climbed in.

"There's a croissant and a coffee back there for you," Alika said, as he squeezed his mammoth bulk into the driver's seat. "Chocolate croissant, black coffee."

"Thanks!" I told him. "You got the croissant right, but not the coffee."

"Cream and sugar?"

I shook my head.

"Not a coffee drinker?" he asked.

"No. Cola drinker. Coke Zero or Diet Coke."

"I have made a note," Alika said, tapping the side of his skull.

"Thought that counts," I said, biting into the croissant. "I appreciate it."

He drove me back onto the Kuhio Highway, across the black steel Hanalei Bridge (and over the Hanalei River, and through the village of Hanalei) and through a quaint little neighborhood to an open beach to … you guessed it … Hanalei Bay.

Although not much effort had been put into naming the place, Hanalei Bay was almost indescribably beautiful. It was a half moon bay, its pale blue waters sparkling like diamonds in the early morning sunshine. The beach sand, at least at this time in the morning, was mostly smooth and undisturbed. The mountains surrounding it were rich with jungle fauna and hugged the bay's outline like a verdant collar. And, reaching out from the beach and into the water stretched a lengthy pier, ending in a widened, roofed gazebo.

"This place is gorgeous," I told Alika, my eyes absorbing the peaceful beauty around me.

"Yes, it is," he agreed.

We stood there a moment, allowing the warmth of the morning sun to hold us in its toasty grip.

"There he is," Alika said, pointing toward the junction where the pier met the beach. "Captain Newton."

We began walking toward a man standing near the shoreline. From a distance, he reminded me a lot of Skipper from Gilligan's Island. The flag blue golf shirt he wore was pulled tautly around his broad-shoulders and barrel chest. He wore a captain's hat, and a pair of what appeared to be Dockers, along with white, slip-on boat shoes. As we drew nearer, I realized the man was much younger than Alan Hale Jr was in Gilligan's prime, and that the jaunty angle of his hat covered an aged scar that ran from his scalp, around his jawline and down into his neck. His skin was tanned a golden brown and I doubted that he'd ever used sunscreen in his entire lifetime.

He looked up at us with a grin as we approached, pushed back his cap, and belted out, "Well, good morning, fellas!"

Alika approached the man and buried him in a huge hug. Newton returned it, slapping Alika's back. I was amazed at how tiny the Captain looked enveloped in Alika's mighty arms.

"And you must be Mr. Heller," said Newton, stepping over and shaking my hand.

"Brace," I said.

"Brace?" Newton asked. "You mean like a polio brace?"

I laughed. "Well, I never heard it described that way, but yes, like a polio brace. And you are the famed Captain Newton, I assume?"

"At your service," Newton said, removing his cap and comically bending at the waist.

I looked down at the tiny inflatable raft that was attached to the rope Newton held in his hand like a leash.

"I hope this isn't your fishing boat," I said.

"Nah, that's just the dinghy that will take you to the fishing boat," Newton said and winked. "Don't make fun of the size of my dinghy." He laughed robustly and clapped me on the shoulder. Then, his gaze turned quizzical. "No equipment?" he asked.

I lifted the binoculars case that hung from my neck. "Just these," I said. "Not so much interested in fishing as I am in sight-seeing."

Newton looked a little disappointed. "Well, you change your mind, I've got equipment on board the Hanalei Hooker."

"Hanalei Hooker?"

"Name of my boat. You know. Hooker, like a fishhook." He laughed again and winked. "Get your mind out of the gutter, Brace!"

I stepped into the water (one of the things I love about my Tevas is that they're waterproof) and then into the dingy. A moment later, Newton pushed the boat out to depth and climbed in. He started the little outboard on the back and we were on our way to the Hanalei Hooker. We passed through a carnival of anchored sailboats, their colorful sails wrapped tightly to masts, and eventually rolled up to an aged but sturdy-looking fishing boat. *Hanalei Hooker* was proudly emblazoned in a cursive font on her backside.

Newton expertly maneuvered the dinghy to line up with a metal ladder that clung to the stern and then indicated for me to climb on up. I scrambled up the ladder with only minimal wobbliness and then stepped back as Newton followed suit. He used a winch to pull the dinghy onto the deck and then maneuvered it as tightly as possible into one corner.

"This is going to be in our way all goddamned day," he said. "But it's the only way to get guests to and from the shore."

"What happens when you have a party of more than one?" I asked.

"Then I choose another dock," he said. "Bad time of year to be going out of Hanalei, anyway. Seas are rough this time of year. Be better this time next month."

"How long does it take us to get to where we can see Hanakapi'ai Beach?" I asked.

"Right around the corner," Newton told me. "Is that what you're here to see? Must be nice if you're too lazy to make the walk to be able to pay someone to drive you out there." He gave that robust laugh and I'm certain he would've clapped me on the shoulder again if I was only closer.

"Something like that," I said. "I'm doing some research for a friend, and the expenses are all his."

"My kind of friend!" Newton laughed. He indicated an ice chest on the opposite side of the deck. "Beer in there, if you're interested," he said. "Nothing fancy, I'm not one for that craft beer shit, but there's Kona in there, which is local enough as far as I'm concerned."

"Works for me," I said, as he climbed the tower and started the engine. I grabbed a Kona out of the ice chest, noting that the only other beer there was Bud Light, and popped the top off with a bottle opener screwed into the side of the deck wall. I took a couple of steps to a fishing chair on the deck, sat down, and took a swig. Not bad. Not good, but not bad.

"Hang on," Newton called from the tower. "We're on our way."

He opened the throttle and the boat pushed forward, seeming to meet a little resistance at first and then breaking free and virtually flying over the waves. I found myself holding the beer tightly in one hand and gripping the plastic chair even tighter with the other. The ride wasn't smooth, and the sea mist was pummeling my face like a sea of tiny stinging bees, but something about it felt fresh and new and exciting.

We cruised at top speed for a while, the growing breeze trying to rip my recently acquired Tracy Vang ballcap right off my head. I wasn't wearing Vang sunglasses, but the wind was apparently after my expensive Ray Bans as well. The lenses were covered with tiny beads of sea spray. Occasionally, we'd hit a wall of water that drove the boat high into the air, and I felt myself becoming weightless for a split second before settling down into the fishing chair again.

The sun beat down on us mercilessly, and I found it difficult to believe it had rained so hard just the day before. Today, there wasn't a cloud in the sky, and I could feel the sun's warmth baking into my skin. I was thankful for the Banana Boat 100 SPF sunscreen I had lathered on this morning as a precaution.

I'd like to say I enjoyed the ride for the 40 minutes or so it took to arrive at our first stop, but "endure" is probably a better word. I couldn't even get another beer because the boat was rocking so hard, I was afraid to get up and attempt to get to the ice chest. The view was beautiful throughout, however, with the lush jungle green and cool blue water offering a mind-boggling panorama of island beauty.

Eventually, I heard the engines begin to die down and the boat slowed and came to a gradual stop ... or at least as close to a stop as it could. Newton came bouncing down the ladder and stood beside me as we stared in toward the shoreline.

"That," he said after a moment, "Is Hanakapi'ai Beach."

The Beach was a slim slice of beige sand tucked between the ocean water and rolling, deep-green cliffs. It was deserted at the moment, and I assumed it was just too early for most of the hikers to have reached their destination there. The beach was surrounded with giant black lava rocks, like those that made up most of Hawaii. The water roiled in turmoil as though boiling and I thought that was one beach I wouldn't want to go swimming in.

"Lotta people drown here," Newton said, as if reading my mind. "Water's too rough to swim in. Rip tides, and such. There's signs but people don't pay much attention. They go in anyway, and a lot of 'em don't make it out."

I opened my binocular case and scanned the beach. It was as deserted as it appeared to be at first glance, and the golden sand there was unblemished and undisturbed.

"So, what do you think?" Newton asked after a moment.

"It's nice," I said. "Very nice. But it's just a beach. What makes it so special?"

He pursed his lips and frowned. "I don't know," he said. "Maybe because it's so secluded? Maybe because you have to hike for a couple of hours to get here? Maybe it's the hike itself, you know? Because it's so pretty."

I scanned the beach through the binoculars again. Sand. Cliffs. Jungle. Lots of jungle. Clinging jungle. This land was always going to be exactly what it was today: a secluded beach. What made it worth $41,000,000? They could build no strip mall here, no high-class resort. I could imagine them putting a fucking Starbucks here because they put fucking Starbucks everywhere, but you'd have to sell a lot of Venti Cappuccinos to recoup forty-one million dollars. Something just seemed dead wrong.

"Maybe I'm just not seeing it," I said to Newton. "Do you mind if we hang here a while? You know, just sit around and see what happens?"

Newton shrugged. "It's your dime," he said. "Or that friend of yours, I guess. We can stay here all day." He shrugged again. "Hey, you want another beer? There's plenty. And let me know when you're ready for chow. I got some tuna sandwiches for us."

I said yes to a beer and maybe to a tuna sandwich and Newton came back with two of each. He handed me a beer and a paper-wrapped sandwich and took a seat in one of the fishing chairs. I sat down in the other one, holstered my beer in the cup holder recessed into the chair and tore the wax paper from around my tuna sandwich. It looked handmade, on whole wheat with pickle relish, and it was better than I expected.

"Make these yourself?" I asked, chewing.

"You bet," he said. "Hell of a lot cheaper if I do it than buy 'em at the store. You like?"

"I do," I said. "Secret family recipe?"

Newton laughed. "Hell, no," he said. "Just tuna, mayo, pickle relish and chopped celery."

"No egg?"

He made a face. "No egg," he said. "I hate boiled eggs. They feel like you're eating an eyeball."

It was my turn to laugh. "I know what you mean," I said. "I don't like boiled eggs, either."

We ate in silence for a moment, the boat rocking beneath us. On the shoreline, the beach did what it had been doing all morning. Nothing. Just being a beach.

I swallowed a mouthful of sandwich and followed it with a swig of Kona. "So," I said. "You been here long?"

"Almost twenty years," Newton said. "Cut a nice retirement and came out here to live my dream job."

"Retirement? You're too young to be retired. What are you, 45?"

"Fifty-three," Newton said. "But I lucked out. Used to work for a company called Amgen. Ever hear of them?"

"Amgen?" I said, amazed. "They're right up the hill from me."

"No shit?" Newton said. "You know Amgen?"

"Yeah, I know Amgen. I live in Ventura. Amgen's like twenty miles away, just up the grade."

"You live in Ventura!" Newton said. "Hell, man, I used to live in Ventura!"

"That's hysterical," I said. "Where about?"

"West end. Near the Avenue."

I knew he meant Ventura Avenue, downtown. "I'm East End," I told him. "Out by Saticoy. That is too funny."

"I loved Ventura," Newton said. "But I always dreamed about running a fishing charter here. Specifically, here, in Kauai. I had stock in Amgen in the early years and, when that company broke big, I was suddenly a rich man. Bought my boat in Long Beach, bought a house in Port Allen and have lived here ever since." He laughed that robust laugh again. "Swear to God, the house cost three times what the boat cost. Ain't cheap to live here, I'll tell you that!"

We finished our sandwiches and our beers and switched from Kona to Bud Light. It tasted surprisingly good in the glaring heat. Bright sun rays reflected off the ocean around us in blinding sheets.

"So, what do you do for a living out there in Saticoy, Mr. Brace Heller?"

I was always careful how I answered this question. Sometimes, it was best to keep my profession a secret. I considered briefly and then decided to go with the truth.

"I'm a private eye," I said. "A detective."

"No shit," Newton said, eyeing me curiously. "A gumshoe?"

"A gumshoe," I agreed. "Shamus. Lots of other words for it out there. Not all of them nice."

"No shit," Newton said again. "So, what are you doing out here?"

"That," I said. "I can't tell you, Captain."

Newton nodded. "I understand, I get that," he said. "But it's got something to do with this beach, eh?"

I shook my head. "I'm not so sure," I said. "I thought maybe it did, but now I'm thinking maybe I was wrong. That's the nature of my business, I'm afraid. You throw everything you find against a wall and see what sticks. This seemed like it would stick, but now I'm thinking it doesn't."

"You mean, because it's just a beach?"

"Well, yes," I said. "I mean, it's literally just a beach. There's no room to build anything, it's miles from the nearest road, and—from what I understand—the hike to get here is no piece of cake."

"Haven't ever done that hike myself," Newton said. "So, I can't tell you."

"Plus, it's my understanding that the government owns most of this," I said, using my hand to indicate the shoreline. "So, it's not like they'd let Hilton or Marriott buy up land to build more resorts on."

Newton drank his beer for a moment, and I could see the wheels of his mind turning. I appreciated the effort, but I wasn't expecting any epiphanies. Everyone always wants to try and help but very few provide any valuable feedback. Still, in the interest of throwing everything against the wall, I let him think.

After a few moments, he turned to me and said, "Maybe the problem is that you're not seeing this from the right angle."

"I'll agree with you there," I said. "But …"

"No, that's not what I mean," Newton said, standing. I followed him to the back of the boat and we stared at the beach for a moment, the hull rocking beneath us.

"What I'm saying," Captain Newton said, indicating the beach using the Bud Light in his left hand. "What I'm saying is that all you can see from here, on this boat, out in the ocean, is a *beach*." He looked at me to see if I understood what he was conveying but my face must have told him I was confused. "You're looking at this from sea level," Newton continued after a moment. "Maybe there's something farther inland, something back away from the beach. Maybe that's where your answer is. You just can't see it from here."

It took me a moment to follow his train of thought but, suddenly, like the proverbial light bulb, the idea flashed into my head.

"That's right," Captain Newton said, apparently catching the expression of understanding coming over my face. "The problem might be that you just can't see it from *here*."

I held up my nearly empty Bud Light can and Newton tapped his against it with a dull *thunk*.

"You, sir," I told him. "May just have something there."

CHAPTER TWENTY

"I need to set up a helicopter tour," I told Alika as I climbed into the Lincoln. My skin was tight with dried seawater, my hair was stiff from ocean breeze and, Banana Boat or no, I was certain sunburn had set in. "Can you help me with that?"

Alika nodded. "I know just the person," he said. "When do you want to go?"

I glanced at my watch. It was nearly three o'clock already. "Probably too late today," I said. "Tomorrow?"

"It will be done," Alika said, starting the car and driving back toward The Cliffs.

He dropped me off and I climbed the stairs to my unit, feeling the effects of sea legs in both my head and calves as I climbed. I took a long shower, rinsing the ocean off me, and made myself a Maker's Mark on the rocks. I know you're supposed to drink Maker's Mark straight but sometimes, you just need some ice.

I sat out on the lanai and watched the ocean for a while. They say you can sometimes see dolphins and even whales at play from the lanai but all I saw was water and more water. I drank another Maker's Mark and ordered a pizza from a gas station up near Akana's office. Normally, a gas station is not the first place I think of when I want pizza, but I'd heard good reviews about this place and wanted to give it a try. They told me my pizza would arrive in about 30 minutes and I figured that was just enough time for another Maker's Mark.

I called Marina but had to leave a message for her. The three-hour time difference was screwing me up. She was probably off at the gym or at yoga or out with the girls for some chit-chat and Chardonnay.

The day on the sea had sucked a lot of energy from me and it was all I could to stay awake until the pizza guy showed up. He handed over my pizza, took my money and bounded back down the stairs. I carried the pizza to the lanai, stopping first to grab a Coke Zero from the fridge, and sat out in the darkness and ate.

Thankfully, the pizza lived up to the hype. It was hot, loaded with cheese and the pepperoni did what pepperoni is supposed to do: Formed into little bowls of delicious pizza grease.

I glanced at my watch. It was barely nine o'clock. Too early for bed but, tonight, I didn't give a damn. I needed some shuteye. Tucking the leftover pizza into the fridge, I stumbled back to my room and collapsed. I was asleep the moment my head hit the pillow.

I awoke some hours later. I don't know how long I'd been asleep. Three, maybe four hours. It was pitch dark in my room. There's not a lot of ambient light at The Cliffs and, when it's dark, it's dark.

But I was aware there was someone in the room with me.

I wasn't sure if whoever it was had made some noise that awoke me, or if there was just a subtle change in the room that made me aware. But, as I lay there in the pitch black, listening acutely for a sound, any sound, that would confirm my suspicions, I felt the intruder's presence as a tangible thing. I knew for certain that someone uninvited had entered the room.

I remained patient and played dead. If there was someone else in here with me, they'd make their presence known soon enough. Whether it was the click of a bone joint or the snick of a hammer drawing back, I'd know they were there and where they were.

I was hoping they didn't have a knife or a machete. Or a brick. Or any other type of silent weapon.

They usually didn't.

The giveaway came as the sound of a drawer being slowly drawn open. It was the nightstand by my head, fifteen inches away. I couldn't have asked for better. First, that sound told me it was nothing more than a common thief in my room. Second, it told me right where he was.

And he was really close to my gun hand.

The revolver Huihui had given me was beneath my pillow and so was my right hand. In one swift movement, I snatched the revolver, swung it in the thief's direction and called out, just like a TV cop, "Freeze!"

Of course, he didn't and, of course, I knew he wouldn't. But what he did do was jump away from the nightstand and, by the time I had swung the blankets off of me and flicked on the light, he had stepped back a couple of steps where his feet stumbled across my discarded shoes and he went down with a crash and an "ooof!" His head collided with the mirrored closet door which banged and rattled with a cacophony all its own and I heard something clatter to the floor beside him.

It was a chrome pistol, probably a 9mm from the quick glance I got of it before I kicked it away under the bed.

"Stay right the fuck where you are!" I told him, pushing the gun down in his face. Based on his sunbaked tan, he was a local kid, early 20s I'd guess, and the look on his face was a cross between fear, surprise, and simmering rage.

I kept my eyes on him as I reached behind me, scrabbled for my phone, and quickly punched one of the numbers I'd entered into speed dial on my first day on the island.

It rang twice, and then there was a drowsy, "Hello?"

"Jay," I said. "It's me, Heller. I've just caught some punk in the middle of burglarizing my room."

There was a slight pause on the other end. Then, "What? Heller? It's three in the morning."

"I'm aware of that," I said. "And I've got an uninvited guest."

This time it sunk in. "On my way," he said, and disconnected.

I sat back onto the bed, never moving the pistol away from the cat burglar. He stared back at me and I could see the options flashing through his brain. He could sit here and wait, and go home with the cops, or he could try to rush me, knock my gun away, and get the hell out. But I held the pistol steadily and he seemed to realize that I wasn't going anywhere. And that meant, neither was he.

"What the hell were you thinking?" I asked him.

"Done it before," he growled with defiance. I could almost sense that he wanted to spit.

"Done what?" I asked. "Robbed someone while they were sleeping? That's a pussy move."

He bristled. "Give a fuck what you think," he said.

"Really, badass? What the hell were you looking for anyway? Cash? Travelers checks? Car keys?"

"None yo' business."

"The fuck it's none my business," I said. "You broke into my room, asshole. You broke into the wrong fucking room."

He glared at me with eyes that were meant to melt steel. It was cute.

Now I heard them, in the distance but obviously coming closer. Sirens screaming in the early Hawaiian morning. The tourists here were going to be thrilled.

"Your ride's almost here," I said, and tensed as the kid made as to move. "Stay put. You won't be the first person I've shot."

"You're going to pay for this," the intruder said in the best English he'd used since I'd met him.

"That's my line," I said, and now I could hear tires screeching as at least two squad cars arrived out front. Then I heard feet pounding up the stairs, then fists on the door. I smirked. There was nothing I could do but wait. If I took my eyes off the punk, he'd make a run for the lanai and either suffer a broken ankle from the fall or die in a hail of police gunfire. If I sat here and waited, they'd break down the door and make their own way in. Either way was going to be loud and unpleasant.

I figured Tracy would pay for the damage to the door.

Sure enough, less than sixty seconds later, I heard the crash of wood and a trio of cops burst into the room, guns drawn. "In here," I called, and sat frozen still.

Jay was one of the first ones in, and he came over to me immediately and grabbed the gun. "What the hell's going on here?" he said.

"Ask Mr. Cat Burglar over here," I said, nodding at the kid. A pair of uniforms had already picked him up by the armpits and were looping his wrists with plastic strips. "I woke up and he was digging through my nightstand." I laughed. "Good thing I sleep with my gun."

"That's bullshit," the burglar said. "He invited me up here. Offered me coke and booze. Said we'd have a good time."

Jay stared at the kid for a moment, then looked at me, and started to laugh. "Boy, did you pick the wrong room to rob," he said.

"That's what I was telling him."

"Get him out of here," Jay said. "I'll take it from here."

The two uniforms dragged my new buddy out of the room, and I heard them descending the stairs. Jay looked over his shoulder, saw the coast was clear, and tossed the revolver to me. "Talk about shitty luck," he said, taking a seat at the desk.

"You got a cat burglar problem here?" I asked.

Jay shook his head angrily. "Not just here. The whole island," he said. "Local crime ring. They bust into tourists' rooms, take their cash, their electronics, their credit cards. Had a guy last week who took all of that and then stole the guy's rental car. We found it a week later, abandoned in the jungle, stripped of every possible thing you can strip a car for."

"Guy get his deposit back?"

Jay laughed. "I doubt it."

"That's some serious shit," I said. "Cat Burglars require a lot of training. It's not easy to break into someone's room and rob them blind without waking them up."

"Been happening all up and down the island," Jay said. "This is the first guy we've caught."

"You think he's part of the ring?"

Jay nodded. "Pretty sure. His buddies were probably sitting outside in a van until they saw your lights go on. They probably skedaddled and left your friend there to take his chances."

"Hopefully, he can lead you to the big guns," I said. "Any gang that's training their team so well that they can break and enter and escape with the goods is nothing to be taken lightly." I stood, headed back to the kitchen, and poured two Makers Mark's neat. I carried them back into the bedroom and gave one to Jay. He nodded thankfully.

"And Cat Burglars are dangerous," I added. "If they're willing to break and enter when someone's at home, they're ready to take any necessary action if they get caught."

"Tell me something I don't know," Jay said, sipping his bourbon. "But so far, so good."

We sat quietly a moment, enjoying our adult beverages and contemplating the happenings of the evening.

"Let me ask you a question," I said. "What do you know about Hanakapi'ai Beach?"

"What do you mean what do I know about it?" Jay said. "It's a beach, just like all the others. Maybe a little harder to get to, but still just another beach."

"So, you don't know about any real estate deals involving that beach? Or development plans?"

Jay shook his head. "Never gonna happen," he said. "Not only is that land all government-owned, but many locals consider it a sacred land. They're not about to let somebody build a strip mall there."

"Yeah," I said. "But that's what they said about Zuckerberg's ranch, too."

I'd read about that in the papers. Facebook CEO Mark Zuckerberg had purchased 91 acres of land on the west end of Kauai and had grand plans for it. But some of the locals had been furious, claiming that the land was sacred and, in fact, had been deeded to some of them through their families. There was a lot of noise made about it, but I never really found out what the outcome was.

"There is that," Jay said. "But I can't imagine the same thing happening there. First of all, that beach is dangerous. You can't swim there. Wouldn't be much of a resort without a beach you can swim in."

"Maybe," I said. "But I can think of several resorts in Mexico that sit on beaches with no swimming, and they seem to be doing just fine."

Jay gave me a look. "Why you asking about that anyway?"

"Just asking," I said. "Trying to find a reason that Mark Akana was killed."

"And you think it has to do with a real estate deal gone bad?"

"I don't know," I admitted. "All I know is that he was in the midst of some giant deal involving Hanakapi'ai Beach and now he's dead."

"You get more on that," Jay said. "I'd like to know."

"I'll keep in touch."

Jay drained the last of his Maker's Mark and I pointed at the empty glass, silently asking him if he'd like another. He declined.

"Gonna go back to bed," he said, standing, and handing me the glass. "You may want to do the same."

"I do," I said. "I've got a helicopter ride tomorrow."

Jay gave me another puzzled look. "Okay, then," he said. "Have a good night."

"You, too."

"Oh, by the way," he said, turning back toward me in the hallway. "You're gonna have to get that door fixed."

"I've got some duct tape in the closet," I said. "That'll hold me tonight. Tomorrow, I'll have Tracy send someone over to give it a more permanent touch."

"Night, Heller."

"Night, Huihui."

I took the empty glasses to the kitchen, rinsed them out and turned them upside down to dry. Then I grabbed the duct tape out of the drawer and did my best to tape the door closed well enough so I could get some rest.

It was nearly 5am, the sun was due up soon. But I went the hell back to bed anyway.

CHAPTER TWENTY-ONE

My "island helicopter adventure" was scheduled for 11:00am and, just to be sure I wasn't late, I set the alarm for 8:30. That gave me time for a shower, a shave, a bowl of Rice Krispies and five minutes to slip into my uniform (shorts, of course, and sandals). Then I peeled the duct tape off the door, bounded down the steps and was almost to the Samurai before I saw the big Lincoln with Alika leaning casually against it, waiting patiently.

"I believe you may be stalking me," I told him as I approached, and he opened the rear passenger door.

"No, sir, it's just coincidence," Alika said. "Mere coincidence."

I settled myself in the back seat and was pleased to find a chocolate croissant and a cold bottle of Coke Zero waiting there.

"Alika, you're a miracle worker," I said, unscrewing the top of the Coke Zero and taking an invigorating pull. "Port Allen, please, sir!"

"Port Allen, next stop," he said. And we were off again.

We headed South, once again along the 56, heading back toward the Lihue airport, (where I had initially landed), and then passed it to the Port Allen airport, a regional airport used mostly for commuter planes and helicopter tours. The weather was gray but at least there was no rain as we cruised smoothly through the lush greenery of Kauai. At times, it was like going through a vibrant, verdant tube. We passed a cattle ranch and an old graveyard and, once again, slowed with the traffic through Kapa'a. We went over a bridge that spanned what looked like the jungle from Jurassic Park (although Alika insisted that movie was shot elsewhere on the island). We passed buildings on stilts, commercial structures that looked like they were cut out of movies from the 1950s, and epic resorts with burning tiki torches on the signs out front, some of them advertising HAPPY HOUR! and $5 MAI TAIS!

I wasn't sure, but I figured a $5 Mai Tai would be mostly fruit juice and water. Still, I was willing to give them a try.

Finally, we arrived in Port Allen and its atmosphere and architecture instantly identified it as a seafaring village. There were shops set up in buildings made of corrugated metal on one side and your standard modern strip mall on the other. Gift shops and tour companies made up most of the businesses there, but I also spotted a Red Dirt T-Shirt Company and a brewery/restaurant called Kauai Island Brewing Company. I was secretly thrilled it wasn't called Hanalei Brewing Company.

Alika drove through the bustling stores and businesses and slowed near a group of about twenty people walking down the street toward the docks. "Snorkeling cruise," Alika told me. "Assuming the water's not too rough. Sometimes, they can only sight-see, never actually get in the water at all."

I scanned the group of would-be snorkelers as we went by and tried to pick out the ones who'd be seasick. The three I'd put money on were a guy who was so white you couldn't tell where his t-shirt ended and his skin began, a doughy woman who wore a bikini top beneath a transparent pink scarf, and a teenaged-boy who looked a little less thrilled to be heading out to sea than his three friends.

Alika turned right and drove to an area protected by a chain link fence. He approached a guard gate and waited patiently while the guard, complete with clipboard in hand and flashlight on hip, came down to greet him.

"Ironwing Helicopter Tours," Alika said, and jerked his head back toward me. "He's got an eleven o'clock appointment."

"Name?"

"Heller, Brace Heller."

"Bryce?"

"No, Brace."

"Oh, yeah, I got him. Go ahead on in."

We drove through the gate toward a tiny little office that reminded me of the old Fotomat shacks, beside which sat a helicopter with a design like that of a news chopper or a traffic copter. It was painted in a dark grey with a diamond plate design and the words IRONWING HELICOPTER TOURS were painted across the side in orange and red letters that were supposed to look as though they were on fire.

Not the best choice of font design, I thought, for a company whose clients might be a little afraid of flying in the first place.

As we drew close to the "Fotomat," the door opened and a woman in a flight suit came out. She was a broad-shouldered and tall and I got the feeling she'd be solid muscle beneath that flight suit. She walked with a confident gait that I admired immediately.

"Jaquet Ironwing," Alika said. "She owns the joint."

"The giant letters on the side of the chopper that spell out her name might have been a clue," I said.

"You are the detective," Alika said.

He brought the car to a halt, and I opened the door before he had a chance to come around and open it for me. By the time I had stepped out, Jaquet was there to greet me.

"Mr. Heller," she said, extending her hand and offering me a charming smile. "I'm Jaquet Ironwing. Alika has told me all about you."

I took her hand and gave it a shake. "Didn't know there was that much to tell," I said, glancing over at Alika. He shrugged.

"Well, it's not like he told me your life story," Jaquet laughed. "He just said he had a friend who was visiting from California who wanted to take a helicopter cruise around the island."

"Specifically, around Hanakapi'ai Beach," I said.

"We'll get you there," Jaquet said, and gave me a sunny smile that made me smile right back. "And we'll see some other things, too. Lots to see here in Kauai!"

I suddenly noticed the logo on the bright pink sunglasses she was wearing. "Tracy Vang?" I said, touching my own pair.

"Tracy Vang!" she said, pleased that I'd recognized them. "My favorite stuff. Local, too. Plus, that guy's a riot. And he's been good to my buddy, Alika, here." She gave him a soft punch on the arm.

"He's been good to me," Alika said, and his face was a work in humble sincerity.

"Have you been up in a chopper before?" Jaquet asked me as we headed toward the office.

"I have," I said.

"Good!" Jaquet said. "Then we'll skip the introductory talk, get all the bullshit paperwork signed and be on our way."

She gave a robust laugh and guided me toward her office. Some people you just like the first time you meet them and Jaquet was one of those. I was beginning to think this would be a pleasant flight.

"I'll be back in a couple of hours, Mr. Heller," Alika said, climbing back into the Lincoln and heading toward the gate.

"This'll just take a couple of minutes," Jaquet said. "Regulations, man, we gotta do it. Then, I'll show you some beautiful sights."

Jaquet was true to her word. The paperwork took maybe seven minutes to complete, and the next thing I knew we were airborne, chopping along the Napali Coast at speed.

"So how long have you been doing this?" I asked Jaquet. I was thankful for the headset she had provided me and which she wore herself. The chopper was loud; there would be no conversation without them.

"Almost ten years," she said. "Set up shop in 2009."

"What'd you do before that?"

"I was a UPS driver," she laughed. "What can brown do for you?"

I laughed. "No offense, but how did you go from UPS driver to helicopter pilot? That's not exactly a straight line."

Jaquet's bubbly giggle sparkled through the headset. "You got that right," she said. "Believe it or not, my grandfather was a famous actor and, when he died, he left me a sizable estate."

"Really?" I said. "Someone I would know?"

"You ever hear of Reggie Blue?"

"The old Western actor?"

Jaquet's smile told me all I needed to know.

"Wow," I said. "I loved that guy. I always thought he out-Wayned John Wayne. And I like John Wayne." I shook my head in disbelief. "He was your grandfather?"

"He was," Jaquet said. "And when he died, he left me a small fortune, enough to move out here to Kauai, buy this helicopter and start up my business."

"How long have you been flying?" I asked.

"Eighteen years," Jaquet said. "I got the bug before Grandpa died. I think that's why he left me so much money. He knew it was my passion and he wanted me to do what I loved."

"That's awesome," I said. And meant it. "What's your favorite Reggie movie?"

Jaquet smiled again, in a quieter, more personal way. "Don't laugh, but it was *The Year Santa Came Home*."

"Really?"

"Well, yeah," Jaquet said. "I mean, he was my grandpa. What would be better than having Santa Claus as your grandfather?"

I nodded. "I guess he kind of was, wasn't he?" I used my palm to indicate the chopper we were flying in.

"Yeah," Jaquet laughed. "I guess he kind of was. What about you? What's your favorite Reggie movie?"

"My favorite Reggie Blue movie?" I said. "Probably *Striations.*"

"The one where he played a modern cop?"

"Yeah, in San Francisco."

"I hated that movie!" Jaquet said.

"He was a tough old bastard in that one," I said. "Shot a lot of bad guys."

Jaquet laughed. "Yeah, that's the problem," she said. "I knew my grandpa. He wasn't the kind of man to go around shooting anyone."

She banked the copter to the right, and I looked out of my side of the glass dome surrounding us. "Down there is the Napali Coast where they shot a lot of scenes for *Jurassic Park*," she said.

"That's wild. It actually looks familiar."

"And a lot of other movies, too. They were shooting *Jurassic Park* when Hurricane Iniki hit. It destroyed most of their sets and some of the scenes had to be cut from the film."

"I'm glad I missed Hurricane Iniki," I said. "Now, Tiki Iniki, that's another story."

"I take it you've been there."

"It's very close to my hotel," I said. "Walking distance. I don't know why I'd go anywhere else."

"They make a mean Mai Tai there," Jaquet said. "Try the Zombie Bowl next time you're there. They light it on fire."

"Sounds like fun."

"The food's pretty good, too."

She straightened out the chopper and pointed ahead of us. "Up ahead. That's what you're looking for. Hanakapi'ai Beach."

I leaned forward in my seat and peered ahead. I recognized the stretch of beach I'd seen yesterday, even though today I was at a very different angle. Thankfully, the clouds had burned off as noon drew near and the day was as clear as a glass of filtered water.

A quick scan, however, told me that I wasn't going to see much more than I saw from Captain Newton's boat. There was the ocean, roiling angrily against the rocks. There was the beach, this time dimpled with the impressions of traveler's bare feet. And there was the jungle, growing up from the beach sand and flowing like a river of vegetation into the mountains of Kauai.

"Not what you expected?" Jaquet asked after a moment, apparently sensing my disappointment.

"Oh, God, no," I said. "It's absolutely beautiful. I've truly never seen anything like this in my life." I laughed. "Well, except in the movies."

"You seem troubled."

"That may be a good word for it."

"Does this have something to do with your case?"

I gave her a look.

"Alika might have told me more than I let on."

"That's okay," I said. "And you're right. I'm trying to prove that someone is innocent of murder, and this beach may or may not be part of it. But I can't figure out why."

"Want to go a little closer?"

"Can't hurt," I said.

She brought the helicopter down a few hundred feet until we were hovering just over tree level. I could see the wind of the blades whipping at the fauna beneath us. We cruised slowly for a bit, back and forth, then again from different angles. There was nothing but beach, ocean, and jungle. There was no telltale fissure that led to the secret headquarters of a James Bond villain, there was no CRA-ZY SHIRTS – COMING SOON sign. There was no in-dication of any traffic above and beyond the Kalalau Trail.

There was nothing to indicate that this was anything but a beach … and was never going to be anything but a beach for a very long time.

"What is it you're looking for?" Jaquet asked.

"I was under the impression that this place was being groomed for something," I said. "Something very big, something very commercial."

"Like what?"

"I don't know. A mall, a hotel, a new Disneyland. I really don't have a clue. All I know is that I had two words and a number: Hanakapi'ai Beach. Forty-one million dollars."

"That's a lot of money," Jaquet said. "But I don't know if it's enough to buy a beach."

I could only nod in frustration. I glanced at my watch. It was nearly 12:30.

"You ready to head back?" Jaquet asked.

"I think so," I said.

I was silent on the flight home as I turned over everything I'd learned so far which, with the exception of why Hilo was hiding, was absolutely goose egg.

Jaquet landed the chopper as softly as a feather and cut the engine. We sat silently in the cabin as the rotors wound down.

"Well, the good news is that, whether or not you found what you were looking for, you know where they shot *Jurassic Park*."

"And I got to meet the granddaughter of the great Reggie Blue."

"That is true."

We both climbed out of the chopper, and I was unsurprised to see Alika waiting for me, leaning against the Lincoln with all the stoicism his plain black suit and dark sunglasses could provide.

"Thanks for riding along, Mr. Heller," Jaquet said, taking my hand again. "I would do this all day by myself but it's better to have good company. Especially *paying* good company," she added.

"Thanks for having me," I told her. I took a few steps toward Alika and then stopped, turned back. "Hey," I called. Jaquet was almost back to her Fotomat booth but stopped and turned back. "Would you like to grab some dinner tonight? There's a place I want to try."

I could tell she was caught off guard. "Umm. I don't know," she replied.

"Look, it's just a friendly thing," I said. "I'm a happily married man." Which wasn't exactly true but close enough to the truth to make a difference. "I'm here in Kauai all alone and I've been wanting to try that Postcards place in Hanalei, especially since Tracy Vang is paying."

Jaquet thought for a moment and then her eyes lit up. "Sure," she said. "How stupid would I be to turn down a meal that a rich man is paying for?"

"Exactly," I said. "I'd offer to pick you up but all I've got is a beat-up Suzuki Samurai."

Jaquet laughed. "You'll wind up upside-down in that thing," she said. "No, that's good. I'll take my bike. 8 o'clock?"

"8 o'clock works for me."

"What's the dress code?" Jaquet asked.

"Hell, it's Kauai," I said. "Isn't it always shorts and sandals?"

She did that addictive laugh again. "It is," she said. "See you at eight." And she disappeared into her booth.

"How was the hunting, sir?" Alika said, opening the passenger door for me.

"Not completely fruitless," I told him. "I mean, hell. I got a date."

CHAPTER TWENTY-TWO

"So, you've been in Kauai all of three days and you're already dating other women," Marina said, shaking her head. "Brace Heller, you dog."

We were FaceTiming on our iPads, and the software wasn't working well with the three thousand miles separating us. Still, seeing her face now, even a little pixelated, was better than not seeing her at all.

"I told her it was purely platonic," I said. "But I can't be responsible if she's weak-willed. I mean, you know how effective my charm and good looks can be."

"Don't I," Marina laughed. "You know, if you take this Jacqueline home tonight …"

"Jaquet," I said. "Ironwing."

"If you take this *Jaquet* home tonight, maybe she can prevent you from being accosted in your room by a complete stranger for a second night in a row."

"That's a good point," I agreed. "Hey, how was your meeting with the budget committee?"

And we talked for a good twenty minutes about the mundane stuff, the boring glue that held all our lives together. It was wonderful. It was almost like being home.

After a while, Marina's tone became serious. "So, Brace, what are you going to do if you can't prove that Malu is innocent?"

"Well, he's not innocent," I said. "Because he *did* rob that guy."

"You know what I mean."

In my room alone, I shook my head. "I don't know," I said. "I can't think that way. I mean, worse comes to worse, I can force Hilo to come forward and tell his version of the story. But it's only his version and he's not exactly the world's greatest witness."

"Potheads usually aren't."

"And where does that leave his parents? I mean, I'd rather a pair of illegal aliens were outed than my friend's son go to jail for the rest of his life for a crime he didn't commit but I'm still going to feel shitty about it. They didn't ask for this."

"They're just as guilty as Malu is," Marina said. "If you're going to use that yardstick."

"Yeah, I guess."

"Well, whatever you do, be careful," Marina said. "You've already had one close call this week."

"You gotta admit that was pretty funny. I mean, that dude never expected to find a gun screwed into his ear."

"It's only funny because of the outcome." I heard her take a calming breath. "You could have been hurt."

"Nah," I said. "That guy was a dweeb."

"Don't underestimate the dweebs," Marina said.

We said our goodbyes, touched our fingers to the screen in an illusion of human contact, and my screen went blank.

It was 7:40. Time to put on my very best shorts and sandals.

And meet my date for dinner.

CHAPTER TWENTY-THREE

Postcards Café is a small quaint cottage that sits on your left as you enter the little village of Hanalei. It looks just like a plantation home that was built in the 1860s. And there's a reason for that. It is, in fact, an exact duplicate of a plantation home that was built in the 1860s, a home that was sadly destroyed (as were Mr. Spielberg's dinosaur sets) when Hurricane Iniki struck in 1992. The building was re-constructed in 1996 and became one of Hanalei's—and indeed Kauai's—premiere restaurant attractions.

Inside, the bare wooden floor is littered with attractive chairs and tables, on which sit Hawaiian flowers and folded cloth napkin tents. The white painted walls reach up to a vaulted ceiling and are adorned with framed antique photographs and long silent guitars and ukuleles.

The restaurant is famous for its fresh meals which are constructed of mostly organic ingredients, including locally grown produce. They serve nothing with meat, poultry, refined sugar, or chemical additives.

In other words, it really wasn't my kind of place, but I knew Marina would want to hear all about it.

I arrived before Jaquet and was led by the friendly *maître d'* to a table in the corner that gave me a perfect view of the main road outside. Our server, who introduced herself as Sandra, came over and poured iced water into two glasses and asked me if I'd like anything else while I waited. I declined, unsure whether Jaquet liked white or red wine or, indeed, any alcohol at all.

A few minutes later, a roar like that of a Tyrannosaur rumbled the very boards beneath my feet and someone on a huge Harley Davidson pulled into the Postcards parking lot. The lot had been full when I arrived, so I had parked the Samurai in another lot a ways down. But there was almost always room for another motorcycle in any parking lot as the Harley rider easily proved.

A few moments later, Jaquet appeared in the front door, her leather jacket zipped up tightly around her and a black motorcycle helmet in her hand. She glanced around the room, caught sight of me and came on back.

"Well, good evening, Mr. Heller," she said.

"Good evening to you, Miss Ironwing," I said, standing and taking her coat and helmet. "Please have a seat."

"Thank you, kind sir."

"And, please, call me Brace."

We sat and Sandra flitted back over, repeating the question about drinks. I looked over at Jaquet expectantly.

She gave me an impish smile. "You said Tracy was paying for this?"

"I am on a full Vang expense account," I said.

"In that case, champagne!" she said happily.

"Champagne it is," I said. "What would you recommend?"

Sandra didn't break stride. "We have a wonderful 2007 MVX Mumm Napa," she said.

"What's the MVX stand for?"

That gave her pause. "You know," she said after a moment. "I don't know. I can find out."

"Doesn't matter," I said. "We'll take one."

And off she went.

"I've lived here for over ten years," Jaquet said, surveying the room. "And I've never eaten here."

"That's what usually happens," I said. "You live close to something nice like this and you never go. Always figure you'll get there another time. And then you never do."

"When I lived in California, it was that way with Disneyland," Jaquet said. "We lived like sixty miles away and we never went. Always said we were going to, and then just never did. The next thing you know, you haven't been there in twenty years, and everything's changed."

"Especially the price," I said.

"Especially!"

"How was the ride up here?" I asked.

"Oh, very nice," Jaquet said. "I love riding my bike and I love the view all the way. You've got the ocean, the jungle, the chickens."

"Yeah, what's with all the chickens?"

"They're part of Kauai!"

"I read that on the plane," I said. "But those little bastards are up way before dawn."

"They crow all the time," Jaquet said. "They don't wait for the sun."

Sandra returned with our sparkling wine and made a production about opening the bottle, letting it pop and sending the cork to the top of the vaulted ceiling. She poured a little in a glass and put it down in front of me.

"No," I said, then, to Jaquet. "You try it."

Jaquet picked up the glass, gave it a little sniff, and then took a sip.

"Oh, yes," she said. "Oh, yes, that will do nicely."

Sandra poured us both a full flute, passed out a couple of menus, and then headed away.

"Do you want to order now?" Jaquet asked quietly.

"Let's not, just yet," I said. "Let's just enjoy our champagne and have a little conversation."

"Is it champagne?" Jaquet asked. "I mean, if it's from Napa Valley, doesn't that mean it has to be 'sparkling wine' and not 'champagne'?"

"Maybe," I said. "But whoever said I play by the rules? I'll call it champagne if I want to."

Jaquet nodded agreement and had another taste.

"Can I ask you a question?" I said after a moment.

Jaquet looked up at me cautiously and then nodded her head.

"So, I take it that you, like most of the island apparently, have known Alika for a long time."

"A long time," Jaquet said. "Long as I've been here."

"And what about Tracy Vang?"

"I know *of* him," she said. "I don't know him personally. Don't think I've ever met him."

"What about his son, Malu?"

"No," Jaquet said quickly. "Don't know him, never met him."

"But you know *of* him as well, right?"

"Well, sure …"

"I don't mean for this to get all weird," I said. "And if it does, just tell me to stop. Because what I'm looking for here is third hand information, and I really have no right to ask. No right to ask you, and no right to intrude on Alika's private life."

"Okay," Jaquet said, and I could see her uncertainty peeking through.

"In all the years you've known Alika," I said. "Has he ever said anything to you about Malu mis-behaving, or about Tracy complaining about Malu mis-behaving?"

"Never," Jaquet said quickly. "Not at all. He's very loyal. He's only ever said good things about Mr. Vang."

"And has he said good things about Malu?"

Jaquet cocked her head and looked off into space. I could see her mind working, her eyes squinting. Then she turned back to me and said, "Absolutely. Said he was a good kid. Said he enjoyed hanging out with him when he took him places."

"And that's your opinion of Malu as well?"

"Well, not exactly," Jaquet said. "I mean, I've only heard about him through Alika. I don't know him personally."

"See, that backs up what I'm thinking," I said. "I don't think anybody knows Tracy Vang as well as his driver. Not only do they spend a lot of time together in that limo, but they've known each other for a long, long time."

"That makes sense," Jaquet agreed.

"And I'm sure Tracy talks to Alika about his troubles just like anyone else would talk to their friends about their troubles."

"Makes sense," Jaquet said again.

"And I know that Alika is probably the loyalist employee in the history of the world but, if he had heard Tracy complain or commiserate about Malu, don't you think he would have said something to his friends, friends like you, maybe only in passing."

Jaquet shook her head slowly. "I'm not sure," she said. "Alika is, like you said, very, very loyal. He may not say anything for fear of embarrassing his boss."

"Maybe," I said. "But he has no trouble talking about the good things, right? I mean, you said he thought Malu was a good kid."

"That's true," Tracy said, taking a sip of her sparkling wine. "But that doesn't really prove anything, either. He may have no trouble talking about the good, but keeps his mouth shut about the bad."

"Yeah, I know," I admitted. "I'm probably just grasping at straws, but that's all I have right now."

"Listen," Jaquet said, sitting forward and clinking her glass against mine. "Are we gonna sit here and talk shop all night, or are we going to get to know one another?"

"I vote we get to know one another."

"Good! Then let's start with you. Tell me how you met your wife. What's her name again?"

"Marina."

"Marina? Like in dock?"

"Kinda, sorta," I said. "And I know I told you that she was my wife, but she's really not. We've just been together for a really long time."

"Okay," Jaquet said. "In some places, that's considered marriage anyway. How long have you lived together?"

"Well, I didn't say we *lived* together," I said, and went on to explain my entire romantic situation.

We talked and we laughed. We ordered an appetizer (seared polenta cakes with a hemp seed crush) and another bottle of wine. After a while, we ordered dinner. Jaquet had the Wasabi Crusted Ahi and I had the Thai Coconut Rice Noodles with Kauai Shrimp Broth. We tasted each other's meal and agreed that both were nothing short of outstanding. We finished our second bottle of champagne and ordered a dessert to split: Banana Bliss—Kauai bananas blended with hazelnuts, pineapple, and a hint of almond with sorbet and a lilikoi drizzle. It was so good we almost ordered a second one, but Jaquet made the mistake of looking at her watch and realized she still had a half-hour ride ahead of her and a six AM charter the following morning.

We paid our bill, I signed for a bigger than normal tip, and I walked Jaquet out to her Harley.

"Mr. Heller," she said. "I want to thank you for a wonderful evening, sir."

"Depending on how long I'm here," I told her, "We should do this again."

"Yes. We should."

I helped her slip into her jacket and, before she lifted her helmet onto her head, she reached up and gave me a lingering kiss on the cheek.

"Been a pleasure to meet you, Brace."

"Pleasure is all mine, Miss Ironwing," I said. "Speaking of which, how the hell did you get a name like Ironwing with a grandpa named Reggie Blue?"

Jaquet laughed and gave me a mischievous smile. "Do you really think Grandpa's name was Reggie Blue?" she said. "He was American Indian through and through."

"What?" I said with mock indignation. "But he was always the cowboy in those Cowboys and Indians movies!"

"It was Hollywood," Jaquet said. "Nothing's real in Hollywood."

She slipped the helmet over her head, tightened the strap around her chin, hopped on the bike and pushed the starter button. The motorcycle roared to life, rumbling the bones in my legs and, with a quick wave, she was gone.

I walked back to the Samurai, started it up, and listened to its bouncy lawnmower purr. Nowhere near as satisfying as a Harley Davidson.

CHAPTER TWENTY-FOUR

I should have seen it before I walked through the door of my room, but my senses were a bit dulled by a few glasses of champagne and the pleasant company of Jaquet Ironwing. Instead, I kicked off my shoes on the landing, walked right through the doorway, and almost ran smack into one of the two behemoth gentlemen who were inside waiting for me.

A third man, barely half as tall as the others and as skinny as a rail sat in one of my kitchen chairs between them.

We stared at each other in complete silence for a moment. "Well, hello," I said at last. "Anyone ever tell you that the three of you almost spell OHIO? All you need is an H."

"Yeah, they said you were a smart ass," said the skinny guy. He wore a pair of oil-stained beige slacks and a filthy sleeveless undershirt. His graying hair was cut close to his head and his skin was the dark almond color of a local who worked on or near the sea. "Sit down, asshole," he continued. "We gotta talk."

"Well, since you asked so nicely." I stepped around the L-shaped sofa and sat on the edge. "What shall we talk about? Maybe about your breaking into my room?"

The little man ignored me. "Hear you had a run in with one of my guys last night," he said, standing and walking toward me. His shirt was even dirtier than I'd originally realized, and his cloying body odor wafted toward me like a London fog. "Hear you had him arrested."

"I didn't have him arrested," I said. "He got himself arrested. It's what happens when you break into someone's hotel room and try to steal their shit."

"He's in jail now," the little guy continued, as if I hadn't spoken. "And that's not good for him, it's not good for me, it's not good for business."

"Well, maybe he should have chosen another line of work," I said. "Barista, maybe. Or car wash jockey."

One of the big guys cuffed me behind the ear with a fist the size of a Volkswagen bug. It took me off guard and almost knocked me off the couch. I recovered as quickly as I could and shot him an angry look.

"Yeah, he don't like it when you talk about a fellow team member like that," the skinny guy said. He reached deep into his left armpit, scratched furiously for a moment, and turned back to me. "One team, one dream."

"I'll make a note," I said, rubbing my ear.

"So, my guy's in jail because you decided to wake up and put the drop on him."

"I held him at gunpoint until the police arrived," I said. "I didn't put the drop on him."

"He says you sucker-punched him."

"What'd you expect him to say? 'Boss, I'm too fuckin' stupid to rob a sleeping tourist?'"

That earned me another cuff on the same ear. I saw stars this time and it felt like there was bleeding. I touched my ear and took a peek. No blood.

Yet.

"I don't think you're understanding me," the skinny guy said. "So, let me make myself perfectly clear. You're going to call the police tomorrow and tell them you were mistaken. My guy wasn't trying to rob you at all. You met him at a local bar, invited him up for a drink, had a few too many and passed out. When you woke up, you forgot where you were, found my guy—your new buddy—drinking from your mini bar, and freaked out. Called the cops before you knew what you were doing."

I stared at him in disbelief. "They're not going to buy that," I said. "That's the most ridiculous story I've ever heard."

Now it was the other behemoth's turn to cuff me. He hit my ear, flat, shocking my ear drum. Pain shot through my head like a needle to the brain.

"Jesus, cut that shit out!" I spat.

"So, are you with us?" the skinny guy said. "You know what to say, right?"

"I'm not saying shit," I told him. "It is what it is. I can't tell the cops I'm recanting my story. That's insane. They'll never believe that in a million years."

"Make them believe it."

"And how the hell do you expect me to do that? Produce video? Because, without it, they're not going to buy a word of this."

The skinny guy screwed up his face, leaned in close and stared into my eyes. "I can see you're not with us," he said.

I was silent.

He stood, dropped his shoulders, and shook his head. "So, we're going to go that route," he said.

"What route?" I asked.

He took a breath and snapped his fingers. Instantly, the two giant thugs took me by my upper arms and dragged me to my feet.

"I need you to know it didn't have to go this way," the skinny guy said. "I need you to know that all you had to do was say 'yes' and play along." He sniffed and sucked at his teeth. "We'll give you another chance tomorrow, but, for now, we're done." He jerked his head at the lanai and the two big guys lifted me like I was weightless and hauled me outside. I twisted and turned and tried to resist but these guys were twice as big as me and stronger than horses. They lifted me up over the railing and, with an effortless push, tossed me over.

It was about ten feet from the lanai to the bushes below and I fell hard into it, back first. I felt a dozen tiny branches rip through my shirt and dig tiny ditches in my skin. A larger branch poked a hole through my shorts and dug into the flesh of my thigh. A flash of pain shot through my right arm, and I twisted it, pulling it free of a branch fork. I tried to take a breath and realized I couldn't; it had been knocked clean out of me.

I tried to roll out of the bush but found myself pinned in place by the various branches and twigs. I felt like a butterfly in a high school lab, affixed to a table while its dissector stared down upon it. My dissector was staring down from the second floor.

"See you tomorrow," the skinny guy said, and let loose a load of greasy tobacco spittle that spattered around my face and neck. He disappeared from my line of sight.

I wriggled around, twisting, and turning, and finally freed myself from the bush. I felt my arms and legs carefully. They were cut and there would be bruises but at least nothing seemed broken. My shoulder hurt where my arm had been twisted back and I could feel a trickle of blood oozing down the back of my neck from a groove that had been carved there.

And, man, was I going to be sore in the morning.

I dusted myself off as best I could, cursing at the number of tears and rips in both my shirt and shorts, and then climbed the stairs back to my unit. The door was propped open but there was nobody waiting inside.

I locked all the doors, stripped off my ruined clothes, and took a quick but painful shower. Afterwards, I slipped into a pair of basketball shorts and my old *Re-Animator* t-shirt, poured myself a Makers Mark neat, and went back onto the lanai and sat down.

I was glad to be on this side of the railing again.

The bourbon burned a delicious trail down my throat and gave me some of my strength back. I grabbed my phone and had dialed half of Jay's number when I stopped and hit the cancel button. Maybe the best play was to keep the cops out of this for now. If I told Jay what had happened, he'd no doubt put a guard on me, and the last thing I needed was a Kauai PD officer following me around as I tried to figure out what was going on with Malu.

Then again, it'd be nice to have a police officer around if Godzilla, Gamera and Scrappy Doo showed up again.

I sat there and drank bourbon and wondered how my evening had gone so wrong so soon. Jaquet had been the perfect company for a lonely traveler; the three gentlemen who'd met me in my room not so much.

After a few minutes, I drained my highball glass and got to my feet. Already, the stiffness and pain were starting to set in. I could hardly wait to see what amazing levels it would reach by morning.

I rinsed out my glass in the sink, set it upside down to dry, and glanced at the clock. It was just after 10:15. Too late to call Jay anyway. I'd try him in the morning.

I hobbled back to the bedroom, pulled back the bedspread and collapsed onto the sheets. The lamp was still on, but I was too goddamn sore to sit up and turn it off. So, I just stayed there, watching the ceiling fan spin, until I finally fell asleep.

CHAPTER TWENTY-FIVE

The pounding rain awoke me at just before 9am. It hammered on the roof and windows like a thousand tiny fists begging to get in. I decided the rain did more than just *fall* in Kauai; it was launched from above as though from a cannon. Its target: the roofs of homes where people were sleeping.

I stirred. The attempt to move generated a throbbing, body-wide pain that felt as though someone had thrown me off the second floor, which, I promptly recalled, they had. After much effort, I was able to pry myself off the bed, zombie-walk to the bathroom and start a very hot shower.

Removing my shorts and t-shirt was like some kind of Torquemada torture but I managed. The sensation of the hot water on my fresh wounds dug daggers into me but the heat did wonders for my sore muscles.

Twenty minutes later, I was toweling off, my muscles limber, and feeling better about the cuts and scratches that adorned my chest, neck and back.

Shorts, a t-shirt and Tevas were applied. Then I called Jay Huihui.

"Jay," I said. "I need a favor."

"Good morning to you, too, shamus," Jay said.

"I need to talk to Akana's wife."

Jay said, "Yeah, no fuckin' way. You might remember she's a widow now. Wife no longer applies."

"I know," I said. "But I need to know what Akana was up to regarding Hanakapi'ai Beach."

There was a suspicious pause. "Okay," he said. "What makes you think Akana was up to anything regarding Hanakapi'ai Beach?"

"I found some information in his office," I said. "Two words and a number: Hanakapi'ai. Beach. $41,000,000."

There was a momentary pause on Jay's end. "So, you're just going to gloss over the part where you said 'found some information in his office.'"

"For the moment," I said. "Yes."

Jay was quiet again. I could picture him trying to decide whether to continue the call or disconnect it and come arrest me. Finally, he asked, "So you think he had some big real estate deal going for Hanakapi'ai Beach?"

"I don't know," I said. "I just go where the clues take me."

"Well, they should take you somewhere else," Jay said. "That place is protected. There's no development going on there. No one can buy or sell it. It was probably just wishful doodling."

"Maybe," I said. "But maybe not. Forty-one million dollars is a hell of a motive for murder."

"You're not wrong," Jay said. "For either a buyer, or a seller."

"So, can you set up an interview with the wife ... widow?"

"You think she knows anything?"

"Hell, I don't know," I said. "That's why I want to talk to her."

"Let me see what I can do," Jay said. "I'll get back to you."

"Thanks, Jay."

I closed the call and went into the kitchen. Cubed some Spam, grilled it brown, and then tossed it in a tortilla with a handful of cheddar cheese. Breakfast of champions. From all the way across the Pacific I heard Marina scream in enraged horror.

Despite the unpleasantness of the night before, and the burbling waterfall of rain this morning, the lanai was still the one place I wanted to be. I wrapped my Spam burrito in a paper towel, grabbed a can of Coke Zero and went outside and sat there, contemplating the gray world around me.

I didn't know if Akana's wife would even talk to me and, if she did, she might either know nothing or just want me the hell off her property. Still, it was worth a shot.

The phone rang and I was surprised to see it was Tracy calling and not Jay Huihui. I clicked the accept button.

"Good morning, Tracy. How are you today, my friend?"

"On pins and needles here, Brace," Tracy said. "Haven't heard from you in a while. Just wondering how things are going."

"The good news is that things are *going*," I said. "The bad news is that I don't have anything concrete yet."

"Do you think you will?"

"Yes."

"Soon?"

"I don't know," I said. "I hope so."

Tracy was silent on the other end. "I don't to mean to bug you," he said after a moment. "I know that you know what you're doing. It's just all the goddamn waiting."

"I know," I said. "I understand."

"Are you any closer?"

"I would like to think so," I said. "But, like I told you, nothing concrete."

It suddenly dawned on me that I'd asked everyone but Tracy, the richest man I knew, about my Hanakapi'ai Beach mystery. When it came to big money deals, didn't it make sense to ask big money people?

"Tracy, do you know Hanakapi'ai Beach?"

"What?"

"Hanakapi'ai Beach. Do you know it?"

I could sense the confusion on Tracy's end. "Of course, I know it," he said. "I've lived here a long time, Brace."

"When's the last time you were there?"

"I dunno. A few years ago. Five maybe."

"Why so long ago?"

"Why? I dunno. I mean, the hike is beautiful, but you can't swim at the beach there. Every year a bunch of people try, and a bunch of people die. I'm a surfer, man, that's not my scene."

"Have you heard about any real estate or development deals going on out there?"

"At Hanakapi'ai Beach? No way. The government would never let that happen."

"Even for $41,000,000?"

"That's chump change when it comes to a beach like that," Tracy said.

"So, you've heard nothing about any deals."

"Of course not," Tracy said. "Because there aren't any. It's impossible. And what does this have to do with Malu, anyway?"

"I'm trying to come up with a motive," I said. "I'm trying to figure out why someone would kill Matt Akana."

"And what does Hanakapi'ai Beach have to do with it?"

"So far, nothing," I confirmed.

"I don't understand."

"You don't have to, Tracy. Let me keep working on it." My phone vibrated in my hand. I glanced at the screen. Jay. "Tracy, I have to go," I said. "Jay's on the other line. I'll give you a call later."

I disconnected the call and clicked the accept button for Jay.

"I got you your meeting," Jay said. "But I have to be present."

"Is that what Mrs. Akana said?"

"No, it's what I said," Jay told me. "The poor lady is understandably distraught, and her children don't want her disturbed. I told them it was police business and we'd be as gentle as we can be."

"And we will be," I said. "The woman lost her husband."

"Yes."

"So, when are you picking me up?"

"I'm driving?"

"You want me to pick you up in the Samurai?"

"Be out front at eleven," Jay said. "Bring your wallet. You're buying lunch."

Chapter Twenty-Six

Jay was waiting in his duty vehicle when I came downstairs at 11. He took one look at the scratches on my face and the bruises on my neck and said, "Rough night?"

"Pretty rough," I said. "Had dinner at Postcards Café."

"Yeah, I should have warned you," he said. "They're pretty tough here when you dine and dash."

I gave him a wan smile. "Actually," I said. "You remember my late-night visitor from a couple of days ago?"

Jay nodded.

"Well, I had a little visit from his boss, and two guys about the size of Buicks."

"What the hell did they want?" Jay said.

"Wanted me to recant my story about the burglar," I said. "Wanted me to tell you that I invited him up, forgot that part, and then freaked out when I woke up and found another man in my room."

"That what happened?"

"Um. No."

"Then why would you tell me that?"

"That's what I told them."

"Where did they leave it?"

"Well, after they threw me off the lanai …"

Jay gave me a side look to see if I was kidding. My expression told him I was not.

"…they promised to come back and see me tonight," I said. "Said they hoped by then I would change my mind."

"Have you?"

"What do you think?"

"I think we'll invite some friends to meet them tonight," Jay said. "See what they think about recanting your story then."

"Sounds like a plan."

The Akanas lived in a modest two-story home on Kahakai Road in Waimea, almost exactly on the opposite side of the island from The Cliffs. With the limited number of lanes available as well as the low speed limits, the drive took us about an hour and a half. Finally, Jay pulled up out front and parked the car at the side of the house.

"I gotta make a call," he said. "Give me a minute."

I stepped out of the car and took the opportunity to call Marina. Her recorded voice told me that she wasn't available to take my call but would get back to me at her earliest opportunity. I glanced at my watch. It was about a quarter to twelve, so 2:45 at home. She was probably in a meeting or something. I smiled. Oh, how Marina hated meetings. I didn't mind them so much, as long as bagels were involved.

Jay completed his call and climbed out of the passenger side. Together, we walked up the sidewalk to the front door.

"Remember," Jay said. "Gentle."

"As a lamb," I said.

Jay knocked on the door and we waited. It wasn't long before it opened, and a young man peeked out. "Lt. Huihui?"

"Yes," Jay said. "And this is my associate Brace Heller."

"My name is Park," the young man said. "I'm Matt's son." I caught a flash of pain across his face as he said his late father's name. "Come on in."

But he didn't move or open the door.

"Listen," he said after a moment. "Mom's been through a lot. I'd appreciate it if you'd make it quick and try not to upset her."

'Of course," Jay said in an understanding tone. "That's the last thing we want."

Park nodded his thanks and stepped back, beckoning us in. The house was pleasant but not opulent. The walls were covered with jaw-dropping photographs of the wonders of Hawaii. Waterfalls, lush jungles, and crowning ocean waves were featured in high-res glory. Park led us through a hallway and into the dining room where a woman sat, sipping at a cup of coffee or tea.

"Mom, the police are here," Park announced.

Mrs. Akana slowly took her eyes off her cup and looked up at us, settling first on Jay and then tracking over to me. Her gaze then dropped back to the cup. Her slow reaction and weary state were evidence of more than grief. I had a feeling there were some sedatives at work as well.

"Mrs. Akana, I'm sorry to bother you again so soon," Jay said. "But we have just a few questions and then we'll be on our way. Will that be okay?"

Mrs. Akana looked up just long enough to nod her approval, and then her eyes went back to her cup.

"Can I get you a cup of tea?" Park asked. "Or water, or something?"

"No, we won't be that long," Jay said, giving me a look that told me to make sure of it.

"Okay, well, then please sit down," Park said. "And let me know if you change your mind." He stepped back and leaned against the sink, taking his own cup of tea and sipping from it as he watched us closely.

I decided to take the lead. "Mrs. Akana," I said gently. "I am so sorry for your loss. As Lt Huihui said, we'll make this quick and then leave you to your family."

Her eyes stayed focused on the cup, but she nodded gently.

"Did your husband ever talk to you about his job? About work?"

Nod.

"Was he recently talking about a particularly big sale?" I asked. "Something bigger than the usual sales he made?"

She thought for a moment, then shook her head. She gave me a sidelong glance that I took as concern.

"Was he anxious recently?" I asked. "Did he seem upset, or excited, in the last couple of weeks?"

Now, Mrs. Akana's head came up and she looked me straight in the eyes. "Why are you asking these questions?" she demanded. Her firm tone was the direct opposite of her drugged appearance. It threw me off guard.

"Well, we're just continuing the investigation," I said, looking to Jay for support.

"Yes," Jay said. "We're still looking into ..."

"Into what?" Mrs. Akana said sharply. "Into what? You know who killed my husband, you know why they killed my husband. What difference does it make what was going on in his business?"

"It's all part of the investigation," Jay said.

"No. No!" Mrs. Akana spat. "You're just trying to find a way to get that criminal out of jail. To blame my husband instead of the man who killed him."

"Not at all," I said.

Jay held up a hand. "Mrs. Akana," he said. "I assure you that's not the case."

She shot him a look that was pure hatred. "Get out," she said. "Get out of my home." She snatched up her teacup, spilling a bit on the white tablecloth. Her hands were trembling noticeably.

"Gentlemen, I think maybe that's enough," Park said calmly. He set his cup on the countertop and used his palm to indicate it was time for us to go.

"Thank you, Mrs. Akana," I said, standing. "And, again, I am sorry for your loss."

"We'll try not to bother you again," Jay said.

"Yes," Mrs. Akana said flatly. "You do that."

We followed Park to the front door, and he held it open for us as we filed out. Then he closed the door behind him and walked with us to Jay's car.

"Sorry about that, guys," Park said. "I'm sure you can understand how upset she is."

"Of course," Jay and I said at the same time. It seemed inappropriate for either of us to tell the other that they owed him a Coke.

"Yeah, Dad never really talked shop with mom," he said. "She would worry too much. Get her hopes up about the bigger deals and what have you."

"Totally understand that," I said. "He didn't want to upset her."

"Yeah. He had a rule that he would never tell mom about any deals until they were done deals."

"Makes sense," Jay said.

"But he did talk to me," Park said. "Said he needed someone to run things past sometimes."

I saw Jay's eyes light up and I knew mine were doing the same.

"And I think I know about the big deal you were talking about," Park said. "Something to do with Hanakapi'ai Beach?"

CHAPTER TWENTY-SEVEN

Jay and I exchanged quick glances and then Jay put his hand on Park's shoulder. "Why don't you step into the car for a moment," he said. "So, we can discuss this."

But Park pulled away. "That's not necessary," he said. "I don't really know that much anyway."

I hoped that Jay hadn't spooked the man. His mother had just accused us of trying to protect her husband's (and his father's) killer and now the police had just asked him to get into a police vehicle. I knew what Jay was trying to do—it'd be better to have this conversation in the

relative privacy of the car rather than out in the open—
but the request had fallen on already suspicious ears.

"No, that's okay," I said in as friendly a tone as I
could manage. "We can talk right here. Tell us what you
know, Park. Anything can help at this point."

There was a pause, and, for a split second, I thought
he was going to turn around and go back in the house.
Instead, he nodded his head. "Well, like I said, Dad didn't
like to discuss business with mom, but sometimes he'd
tell me things about the deals he had going down. Especially the bigger ones."

"Were you involved in the business?" Jay asked. He,
too, was using his best friendly conversational tone. I was
pleased that he had picked up on the atmosphere here.

"Oh, no," Park said. "I live in L.A. I write comic
books. I never really had any interest in taking over the
family business."

"Go on," I said.

"Well, during the past few weeks, Dad was working
on something that he said was big. Really big. Perhaps the
biggest deal he'd ever been working on."

"Did he tell you what?"

"He said some big conglomerate was looking to buy a big chunk of Hanakapi'ai Beach. Open some sort of shipping center there or something."

"How was that deal supposed to work?" Jay asked. "That land all belongs to the Hawaiian government."

Park shrugged. "I don't know" he said. "But Dad said he thought he'd figured out a way. And his chunk of the sale, his commission, was going to be at least a couple million dollars."

"Did he say how much this sale was, exactly?"

Park shook his head, his eyes tilted to the right as he thought. "It was some crazy amount," he said. "Like forty million dollars."

Bingo. Hanakapi'ai Beach Project. $41,000,000.

"Did your father tell you who the conglomerate was?" I asked. "Did he mention any names to you?"

"That was the weird thing," Park said. "I asked, but he would never tell me. Just said I didn't need to know."

"Did he ever say anything about where the deal was? You know, status-wise?"

"Last I heard," Park said. "It was still a go. Dad said there were hoops he had to jump through, but he thought the deal could be done."

"Thanks, Park," Jay said. He reached into his windbreaker and came out with a business card. "You think of anything else, you let us know.'

"Will do, Park said, but he didn't take the card. "You can keep that, lieutenant. I've already got one."

Jay nodded. "Of course," he said.

"Park, I can't thank you enough," I said. "This has been a tremendous help."

I shook his hand, Jay shook his hand, and Park went back to the house. Jay and I climbed into the car.

"The plot thickens," Jay said.

"It do," I confirmed.

"You thinking what I'm thinking?"

"Probably."

"I'm thinking," Jay said. "That your little visit from the three bad guys last night might have less to do with protecting a cat burglar than it does with your sticking your nose where it don't belong."

"Well, shit," I said. "I wasn't thinking that at all. Thanks for putting that little worm in my brain. I'll be looking over my shoulder everywhere I go now."

"Probably a good thing," Jay said. "What were you thinking?"

"I was thinking we need to get back into Matt Akana's office. Get a closer look at his files."

"That would be nice," Jay said. "But that's not gonna happen. No judge is going to grant us a warrant without evidence, and we got nothing. And there's no way Mrs. Akana's going to grant us access. You heard her."

"Maybe Park can convince her."

"Maybe, but is that worth it? That's a lot of effort to maybe, probably, find nothing."

"So where do we go from here?"

"Well, I can talk to some of the local politicians," Jay said. "They would have to be involved with any deal that involved Hanakapi'ai Beach."

"Politicians?" I asked. "What are the odds they'll even talk to you?"

"Between slim and none," Jay said. "And slim didn't come to town."

"Cute. So, what's the point?"

"Can't hurt," he said. "And I think we need to put some pressure on that local crew."

"The guys that dropped by last night?"

"The same," Jay said. "If it's the crew I think it is, they work out of a body shop in Nawiliwili. I may drop by and have a little conversation with them."

"Why don't you hold off on that," I said. "If they are really planning on paying me another visit tonight, it gives me a little ammo. Maybe I can glean a little information from Mr. Smelly."

"Or maybe you can get your ass kicked again."

"Quite likely," I said. "But you're just a phone call away, right?"

"I'll be closer than that."

We were quiet for a moment.

"So, what do we do now?" I asked.

"What do you mean what do we do now?" Jay said. "I believe I told you that you were buying lunch."

"Of course," I said. "How could I forget? What have you got in mind?"

"There's a sushi place I like in Hanalei," Jay said. "You into sushi?"

"I'm fine with it," I told him, "As long as there's enough soy sauce."

"You're such a *haole*," Jay said, shaking his head sadly. "I'll make sure there's enough soy sauce."

"In that case, let's eat." I said.

And, once again, we were off.

CHAPTER TWENTY-EIGHT

I asked Jay to drop me off at The Cliffs so I could pick up the Samurai because I had some detecting to do after we finished lunch. We agreed to meet at a place called Bouchons because Jay liked the sushi there. I wasn't the biggest fan of sushi, but I figured it'd be better to eat raw fish at a restaurant that was near the ocean rather than somewhere like Las Vegas, where sushi was popular, but the nearest ocean was almost 300 miles away.

Lunch was better than I expected. Jay made me sample several types of sushi I never would have tried on my own and, for the most part, I enjoyed it. They can keep the eel, however. It was tough and had a strong, bitter flavor I didn't like at all.

Jay said I was just being a baby.

When we were finished, I gave the server my credit card and was glad that this meal was going on Tracy's expense account. The sushi here was better than I expected, but it wasn't cheap.

"So, here's the plan," Jay said as the server returned my credit card and receipt. "There will be four of us at your place tonight, starting at about 5:30."

"That makes sense," I said. "There's no way those guys are coming out when it's still light."

"Exactly," Jay continued. "We'll all be undercover, sitting at different places in the parking lot, so we'll know when they arrive."

"And when do you pop them?"

"We're going to wait five minutes after they enter your room," Jay said.

"Five minutes is enough time for them to put a bullet in me."

"We've got faith in your conversational skills," Jay said. "Keep them busy until we get there."

I wasn't exactly happy about the five-minute delay—it took them just about five minutes to throw me over the railing last night—but Jay was playing it smart. Five minutes was enough time to catch the intruders red-handed.

We said our so longs and I headed back to the Samurai. Bouchons wasn't far from Ke'e Beach, where the Kalalau Trail began, and I thought maybe I'd sit there a bit, just watch the comings and goings, and see if there was anything I could learn.

I thought briefly about trying the trail myself, but it was a hot day and that sounded like a lot of work. I was certain that I'd see nothing I hadn't already seen on my ocean and helicopter excursions. Plus, I had a belly full of sushi that would slow me down.

So, I took the serpentine 560 highway through the expansive vegetation and over the single lane bridges and past the stilted homes. The view on my right was breath-taking, the glorious turquoise water and golden sand beaches threatening to take my attention off the mechanics of driving. The left side wasn't much better, being either sharp cliffs that led up to perched tufts of greenery or thick carpets of jungle, too dense to see far into.

It was gorgeous enough almost to make me miss the fact that I was being followed by a black BMW.

Unless there was someone lying down or hiding in the back seat, there were two of them, the driver, and his passenger. Both wore black suits with thin black ties and what looked like Ray-Ban sunglasses, as best I could see in the rear-view mirror. They looked like they just stepped out of *Reservoir Dogs*, and that gave me no comfort.

I drove calmly for a few moments, keeping an eye on them, watching them make every turn I did like a carbon copy.

Maybe I'm being paranoid, I thought. The fact was that there was only one road along this coast of Kauai. If they were going to Ke'e or Tunnels Beach, there was literally no other way they could go.

But these guys didn't look like they were dressed for the beach, and the way they kept at least three or four cars' space behind me was very methodical, leading me to believe this was more than just a coincidence of one road.

A parking lot appeared on my right, and I turned in. There were two story residential units there (probably time shares or hotel rooms), a restaurant in front of me and, to my left, a small building with a sign proclaiming HANALEI DAY SPA.

Seriously? Weren't there enough things called Hanalei on this end of the island already?

I parked in a space near the restaurant, climbed out of the Samurai and approached the restaurant. Thankfully, it wasn't named the Hanalei Steakhouse, but rather Mediterranean Gourmet. I tried the door, but it was locked. A sign in the window announced they were open at 4pm. I glanced at my watch. 3:30. Timing is everything.

I casually turned and scanned the parking lot. Sure enough, there were my buddies in the BMW, parked at the opposite end of the parking lot from the Samurai. I couldn't see if they were still in the car or not because of the other cars parked around them. But I didn't see them walking around either. And they would have stood out, with their Quentin Tarantino suits and all.

There was a gift shop next door, so I decided to browse for a moment. Maybe find Marina a carved coconut monkey or a plastic hula girl for her dashboard. I looked around casually, chatted with the friendly cashier there, and thought about buying a hot dog from the snack bar in the back. It was one of those pre-packaged ones that you heat in the microwave, so I passed.

I went back out to the Samurai and started it up. The BMW was where they'd parked it, but I still couldn't see if anyone was inside without being totally obvious. I backed out of the parking space, headed to the main road, and turned right toward Ke'e.

A few moments later, the BMW appeared in my rear-view mirror and settled behind me. That was good news. That meant their orders were just to follow me, not to kill me.

At least not yet.

The parking sucks at Ke'e, there's just no two ways about it. It's basically a cramped rectangle with parking on the edges (NO PARKING ON PAVEMENT, the sign insists) and the odds of finding a space when you want one are basically the same as being chosen to command a NASA flight to Mars.

I was in someone else's Suzuki Samurai with an expense account. I could drive around all day until a spot opened if I had to.

But I lucked out. As I entered the parking rectangle, I saw the reverse lights of a rental car flash on five spaces in front of me. I stopped and waited, much to the chagrin of the driver behind me, also in a tourist vehicle, who bleated his horn as though expecting me to move on so he could take the space.

Yeah, fuck you, buddy.

The car in front of me finally pulled out of the spot and I slipped in, getting a kick out of the middle finger the guy behind me threw as he passed. Tough guy, gutsy enough to flip me off as he drove past. The ones you have to worry about are the ones that do it to your face.

A couple of other cars passed behind me and then there was the BMW. The two guys inside made a production of not looking my way as they drove by. If there was any doubt that they were following me—which there wasn't—their dramatic abilities, or lack thereof, proved it for sure.

I watched them drive to the end of the rectangle, make the U-turn there, and head back my way. Once again, they drove by like mannequins, their eyes staring straight forward, the hands on the wheel not moving. This time I got a good look at the driver. He was clean-cut and shaved, and the suit he wore (while being about sixty years out of fashion unless you're one of the Blues Brothers) was neat and pressed.

That was in complete juxtaposition with the men who had met me the night before. The filthy pants and stained undershirt didn't match up with the professional appearance of the guys in the BMW. They probably weren't part of the same crew. So, who the hell were they?

I sat in the uncomfortable driver's seat and all thoughts of the Kalualu trail vanished. Who had sent these guys to follow me and what were they hoping to learn? I was sure it wasn't Pops and the two human mountains that had come to my room the previous night. What had I triggered to earn the attention of someone else as well?

I decided to see if I could find out.

I waited until the BMW returned and I didn't have to wait long. Apparently, the driver had gone back down the road, found somewhere to flip a U, and then returned to the Ke'e Beach Parking lot. The BMW passed slowly behind the Samurai, again with the passenger's eyes staring intensely straight forward. I immediately started my car and shifted into reverse. As I hoped, the car behind the BMW came to an abrupt halt, thrilled to find an opening spot, and I backed out. I shifted into first gear and accelerated. Within moments, I was behind the BMW.

What's that cliché phrase? The hunter had become the hunted.

Although they didn't turn or stare into the rear-view mirror, I could sense from their body language that the boys in the BMW knew I was behind them and that it was now me following them. And there was nowhere for them to go. The 560 is a two-lane highway with many stretches that are only one lane. Unless they turned off somewhere as I had earlier at the Hanalei Day Spa, I could follow them all the way back to their headquarters. Now that they knew I was aware of them, and that I was the one doing the following, my bet was that they'd just keep driving.

We drove on. I could see the tenseness in the driver's shoulders, and I stayed close, turn after turn. The passenger sat completely still, and, for a moment, I wondered if he was one of those inflatable people that drivers in L.A. use to get into the diamond lanes. We came to a stop at a one-lane bridge, and I sat close behind them, waiting for the oncoming traffic to pass. Then it was our turn.

But the BMW didn't budge. A moment passed. The car behind me tapped its horn. I shrugged toward the rear-view mirror. Finally, a car coming the other direction got tired of waiting and started across the bridge.

And then the driver in the BMW put the hammer down and the car rocketed across the bridge, swerving at the last moment to barely avoid the other oncoming car. There was a screech of brakes and I heard someone shout

"Asshole!" as the other car continued toward me, blocking my way.

There was no way I was going to catch a BMW in a Suzuki Samurai. Whoever Mr. Pink and Mr. Blue were, they were lost to me now.

For the moment, at least.

CHAPTER TWENTY-NINE

It was just before 5pm when I got back to The Cliffs. Jay and his team would be arriving in about thirty minutes and my other guests were expected sometime after dark. It was going to be an interesting evening.

I opened the door, took off my shoes, and considered taking a shower. There would be time for that later. I went to the fridge, made a quick Spam sandwich, and grabbed a Coke Zero. I also took a moment to pour a couple fingers of Makers Mark.

I sat down at my place on the lanai and watched dusk bring down its shadowy curtain. There was something magical about this place and I couldn't wait to bring Marina over here. She would love everything about Kauai.

As if on cue, the phone rang, and I glanced at the number. The face of my phone said CONFERENCE and there were two numbers listed. One of them was an 808 number I didn't recognize.

The other was Marina's.

An electric shock fired through me, and my whole body felt numb. I punched the ACCEPT icon.

"This is Heller," I said.

"Mr. Heller," said a voice I remembered, and my blood went stone cold. "I'm sure you remember me."

It took me a moment to find my voice. "Yeah, I remember you," I said. "You're the short skinny fuck with the bad B.O."

The voice on the other line laughed humorlessly. "So, you do remember," he said. "Do you also remember what I asked you to do?"

"I do."

"And did you do it?"

"No," I said. "I'm not going to do it."

Another dry, humorless laugh. "Well, I have someone here on the other line who might sway you to change your mind," he said.

And, for a moment, I heard Marina say my name before she was abruptly cut off.

The icy feeling in my blood became white hot.

"I'm sure you recognized that voice," Body Odor said. "And so, this is my new offer, my latest offer, my last offer, Mr. Heller. Either you recant your story and convince the Kauai police that you were mistaken and that my friend was there as your guest. Or you come home to an empty house."

I was quiet a moment, trying to keep control of the mad fury that was pounding in my veins.

"Okay," I said. "Now it's your turn to listen. I'm going to give you one chance to walk away from this. One chance to call off your minions and walk away from this clean. You've crossed a line here that cannot be uncrossed, and this is your one and only chance to walk away." I stopped and took a stabilizing breath. "Do you understand?"

The humorless laugh came again, this time in almost a whisper. "I'll gladly walk away," the skinny man said. "Once you're cleared my friend with the police. You've got three hours."

And the line went dead.

I sat there on the lanai, the Makers Mark, the Coke Zero, the Spam sandwich forgotten in front of me.

And then I called Puño.

# # # # #

It was pitch black out on the lanai. I hadn't bothered to turn on any lights. I hadn't moved from my chair. Flies buzzed around my stale sandwich. Around me, I could hear the sounds of other guests having dinner, laughing at bad jokes, and generally being alive. But I sat in the dark and waited.

I had called Jay off right after I had talked to Puño, and he had pulled his team. He was uncertain at first, concerned that perhaps the bad guys were already at my unit when I got home. I assured him that was not the case.

And I sat in the darkness and waited. My mind was as black as the night around me. No thought crossed my mind. I simply waited.

An hour later, the phone rang. Puño.

"It's done," he said.

"Marina?"

"She's fine. A little shaken. She's going to stay at my place tonight."

"How many?"

"There were two of them, one at the door, one in the room with her." There was a serious pause. "It was easy."

"I'm going to need you to come out here," I told him.

"I know," he said.

"Can you put together a team?"

"Hard," Puño said. "Difficult to get guns from Point A to Point B."

"I understand," I said. "I think I can get some weapons here."

"I'll bring the beefcake," he said. "You bring the hardware."

"Deal." I sighed. "Can I talk with her?"

"Of course."

And he handed the phone to Marina.

"Baby, you all right?" I blurted before she even got to the phone.

"Yes, I'm fine," Marina said. "But, Brace, I was so scared." She took a deep breath. "Fuckers."

"I know," I said. "You weren't meant to experience that. Ever. I'm sorry. And you're safe now. Puño is with you."

"Puño …"

"I know," I said. "I asked him to."

She was silent on the other end. Then: "Are you safe over there, Brace? Is this over?"

"Not yet," I confessed. "But it will be very soon."

We sat three thousand miles away from each other, each quiet on the phone.

"Can you take a few days off?" I asked her. "Sick leave or something?"

"Yes," she answered, breathlessly and quickly.

"Puño's coming out here to meet me," I said. "I want you to come with him."

"Yes," Marina said. "I want to."

"We'll set it up," I said. "I'll see you tomorrow."

"I love you, Brace," Marina said.

"I love you, too."

I disconnected the call and felt a wall of concern fall away from me. I snatched up the Makers' Mark and downed it in one gulp.

Marina was coming to Kauai tomorrow, and it would do me wonders to know she was safe.

But Hell was also coming to Kauai tomorrow, in the guise of Puño and his gang, and I knew a guy in a dirty undershirt and his pack of cronies who had burgled helpless tourists for the last fucking time.

CHAPTER THIRTY

Their flight landed at Lihue airport at just after noon. I was waiting outside when they arrived.

Marina saw me first, her eyes lighting up as she ran toward me and I enveloped her in my arms. Puño was behind her, Marina's luggage tucked into the crook of one arm like it was a bag of groceries, and he gave me a half-smile that told me he was glad to see me but was ready to take care of business as well. Behind him were three other Mexican guys I didn't know. The fact that Puño knew them, and trusted them, was enough for me. We all piled into the Lincoln, pushing its seating capacity to the limit, and I introduced them to Alika.

We drove to Princeville in near silence, with only Puño taking a moment to introduce me to his friends. There was Miguel, a suave, compact but well-built man who smelled of aftershave or cologne. There was Rigoberto, whose broad shoulders and muscular arms took up quite a bit of space in the car. And there was Jesus, who looked nothing like his namesake but more like Danny Trejo of *Machete* fame.

Alika dropped us off at The Cliffs and we went up to the room. "Marina and I are back there," I said, pointing to the main bedroom. "There are two beds upstairs, so two you of you can sleep up there."

"Miguel, Rigo, that's you." Puño said.

"One of you will have to take the couch," I said. "I don't know what to do with the other."

"Jesus, you take the couch," Puño said. "I'll sleep on the balcony. Gotta be nice, all this Hawaiian air."

"You sure about that?" I said. "Won't your snoring wake the neighbors? Not to mention the dead?"

"Probably," Puño said. "But once they see me, who's going to complain?"

"Good point," I said. "By the way, it's not a balcony, it's a lanai."

"Whatever."

The men went about their business, setting up their areas. Marina looked up at me. "I'm starving," she said.

"Plenty of food in the kitchen," I told her. "Tracy put enough in there for an army."

"Good thing," Marina said, looking around.

I walked out to the lanai where Puño stood, looking out over the ocean.

"Beautiful, isn't it?"

"Exactly how I pictured it," Puño said. "You know, from the magazines and TV."

"Almost doesn't seem real," I said.

We watched the sun dance on the ocean. Sparkling little diamonds winked back at us.

"You set up the armory?" Puño asked.

"Not yet," I said. "But we have an appointment at three."

He looked at me curiously. "With who?"

"Man by the name of Leon Huihui," I said. "He's the uncle of a police detective I'm working with here."

"Why we meeting with him?"

"He's an arms collector," I said. "Probably has some stuff we can use."

"And your police friend?"

"Jay."

"Jay. He's okay with this? Getting guns from his uncle?"

"Hell, man," I said. "He set it up for me."

Puño nodded toward the kitchen. "'Cause of what they did to your lady?"

"Partly," I said. "And partly because of what they've done to his island."

Puño nodded again. He understood.

"We got time for a meeting before we go shopping?" Puño asked.

"Sure. Let your guys get settled in and then we can sit down and discuss our options."

"Only one option," Puño said. "And you know what that is."

"I know," I said grimly.

"But we gotta have a game plan," Puño said. "Won't take long."

"Can't," I said. "You know they'll be coming after me tonight."

"Which is why we got to get to them first."

"Exactly."

Marina came to the sliding door with an exasperated look on her face. "There is more fucking Spam in there than I've ever seen in my lifetime," she said. "Please don't tell me that's all you've been eating."

"Maybe," I said to Puño with a grin. "You should have left her back home."

CHAPTER THIRTY-ONE

Alika picked up Marina at 5pm. She wasn't thrilled at being shuttled off to another address, but we couldn't leave her here with the possibility of the Body Odor gang showing up while we were gone and the only place I knew she'd be safe was the Vang Estate. Tracy was over in Honolulu doing some promotional nonsense and wouldn't be home until later, but he promised me that his staff would be ready, willing, and able and that anything Marina needed she'd get.

We were ready when Alika came back for us at 6pm. We climbed into the back of the Navigator, a little worse for space due to the hardware we'd borrowed from Leo Huihui's impressive collection. If we got pulled over for any reason, we were all going to jail. There was no way to explain the amount of artillery jammed into that little cabin.

We were silent as we drove south to Nawiliwili. There was nothing to be said that hadn't been said already. We were ready.

As ready as we were ever going to be.

I glanced out my window at a yellow traffic sign on the side of the road. BEGIN RUMBLE STRIP, it read. I knew that it meant the deep notches carved into the road that rumbled throughout your vehicle to wake you up or as a reminder to stay in your lane. But I couldn't help but feel it was also a warning to those of us in the car, those of us heading off into battle.

There was a McDonald's near the harbor where the body shop was located and Alika pulled the limo into the parking lot there.

"Big Mac, anyone?" I asked.

No one laughed or even responded. It was neither the time nor the place.

The rear door opened, and Jay Huihui squeezed in, having some trouble closing the door behind him. "Make some room, please."

Everyone wriggled around until Jay was able to shut the door. He settled in, and then looked around the back at each of us.

"Okay," he said. "Here's the deal. I just drove past the shop a few moments ago and it seems they're all there."

"So, they haven't headed up to Princeville yet," I said. "To see me."

"Correct," Jay said. "But that doesn't mean they won't soon. So, we have to do this quickly."

"Agreed," Puño said.

Jay turned around toward Alika. "Alika, there's a parking lot for the dinner cruise just down the road."

"I know it."

"Go in and park there, as close to the chain link fence as you can."

"Got it."

Jay turned his attention back to us. "That fence is right next door to the body shop. We'll go in through the gate there, come in from the rear."

"Sentries?" Puño asked.

"None that I saw," Jay said. "But keep your eyes open."

Alika started the car, pointed its nose down the road toward the harbor.

"You get hold of your guy?" Jay asked me.

"Yes," I confirmed.

"When will he be here?"

"Ten minutes after I make the call," I said.

"Jesus, how the hell does he do that?"

"I don't know," I said. "I don't want to know."

"Probably best."

Alika pulled the Navigator onto a gravel parking lot and drove down toward a large, corrugated steel building. He stopped at a chain link fence that blocked the sunset cruise parking lot off from the body shop. There were lights in the body shop window. Dusty broken cars littered the yard behind the shop, their shattered windshields and headlights reflecting the hovering moon's brightness.

Alika stopped. "This good?"

"Perfect," Jay said. He looked again at each of our faces. "Everyone ready?"

Their flat easy stares told him all he needed to know.

"Let's go."

We piled out of the car and moved over to the gate. Jay had already used a bolt-cutter to cut through the lock and all we had to do was simply open it. We slipped through one by one, closing the gate behind us.

We crept closer to the wall. Inside, the voices of men could be heard. We couldn't decipher their words, but it was obvious there were several of them.

The POP of a silenced shot went off behind me and I flinched. I turned to see Miguel holding his pistol toward the sky, a stream of smoke trickling from its barrel. Ten yards in front of him lay a body, a black pool of blood growing beneath it, the moon reflected there as well.

One down, I thought, and regretted thinking it. I stepped over and glanced down at him. Nobody I knew. I kicked the gun beside him beneath a dumpster.

Silencers aren't truly silent but work well enough so that someone who hears it at first thinks that the sound must be something else. Fireworks, maybe. Their first thought is *that couldn't possibly have been a gunshot.*

I crept around toward the rear entrance of the shop and waited, the team following close behind. As I expected, a moment later the back door opened and one of the giants that had thrown me off the lanai stuck his head out, looking for his partner.

I shot him in the forehead and he dropped like the proverbial rock. The sound of his body as it fell against the steel wall was like a car wreck and we knew that any element of surprise was gone.

We ran forward into the building, streaming over the enormous carcass of Giant #1 and spilling into the building. I saw something move off to my right and there was a flash beside me as Jay took the shot, dropping a man holding a .45. There were cars in various states of repair all around us, none of which looked as though they'd been worked on any time recently, and a battered steel workbench dead ahead.

Body Odor sat at that workbench, a single exposed lightbulb dangling above his head. On the table in front of him was a .45 pistol, probably a Colt. The expression on his face wasn't one of fear but rather of mild surprise.

Someone beside me fired a shot and I looked over my shoulder to see Puño pointing his weapon toward a catwalk near the ceiling. A split second later, a body fell to the ground with a pumpkin-like splat. I turned my attention back to Body Odor.

He gave one of those humorless laughs and then tried to smile. It was more like a knife wound with teeth.

"So, I assume this means you're not going to accept my offer?" he said, and laughed again.

"I told you," I said. "You crossed a line you can't uncross. You took my *wife*. I gave you the opportunity to walk away."

The only sound in the building for a few moments was the steel walls trembling in the wind and the creaking of leather and gear from the men around me.

"So, what are you going to do now?" Body Odor said after a moment. "Kill me in cold blood?"

"Yes."

"And what good will that do you?" Body Odor said. "Do you think that'll stop everything? Do you think they won't keep coming after you?"

"Don't care," I said. "*You* won't."

Body Odor shook his head sadly. "So foolish," he said.

And snatched for the gun on the table.

I pulled the trigger twice, putting one shot through his face and the other in his chest. The .45 fell out of his dead hands and clattered to the floor. He fell back into the chair like a man who'd fallen asleep at the office, the mask of red on his face and the red bloom on his chest the only indications otherwise.

We stood there a moment, listening to the sounds of the building.

"Make the call," Jay said to me. "Get your guy …"

We all ducked as four gunshots exploded behind us. I turned to see Giant #2 standing there, a sub-machine gun gripped in his mighty arms, his face a study of pained surprise. A split-second later, he fell clumsily onto his face, like a slab of beef dropped from a meat hook.

Behind him stood Alika, a smoking 9mm in his hand. He stood there a moment, breathing, and then lowered the pistol. "I got your back," he said weakly.

I nodded my gratitude.

"Make the call," Jay said anxiously. "We got to get this shit going."

I pulled out my phone and dialed a number that I was forbidden from ever writing down or storing in my phone. It was answered on the very first ring. "Good evening," a reedy voice with a New Orleans' accent said, "How may I be of assistance?"

"Gruber, it's Brace Heller."

"Are you ready?" Gruber replied.

"I am," I said. "We are at the location discussed earlier."

"Near the harbor," Gruber said.

"Yes," I said, thinking once again how much the man sounded like the late Vincent Price.

"Interior or Exterior?" Gruber asked.

"Both. Exterior minimal."

"Dead count?"

"Five. Two of them rather large."

"No unfriendlies on site?"

"Just the dead ones."

"My team will be there in seven minutes," Gruber said. "Can you maintain until then?"

I looked at Jay. He nodded. "Should be no problem," I said.

"Forty-two thousand," Gruber said. And the line went dead.

"We're good," I said to Jay. "Let's get the hell out of here."

We all went back out the rear entrance and climbed into the Navigator. Minutes later, we were back on the highway, heading toward Princeville. Not a word was spoken. Despite what they say in the movies, killing is never easy, even for those whose careers depend on it. It takes a grim toll. I had a hunch that there wouldn't be a full bottle of liquor left in the house by morning and I, for one, would be responsible for a lot of it.

I also thought briefly about the $42,000 Gruber charged for a scrubbing. Once again, I was glad my friend Tracy was footing the bill.

CHAPTER THIRTY-TWO

Once back at The Cliffs, we each adjourned to our individual areas. I went into the kitchen first, grabbed the bottle of Makers Mark, and headed off to my bedroom, closing the door behind me. I knew the others were at their places, too: Puño on the lanai, Miguel and Rigoberto in the upstairs bedroom and Jesus on the couch. Each would be going through their post-mission ritual, which consisted of either getting blind-ass drunk, praying through the night, or meditating until morning. Everyone had their own way with dealing with what had to be done.

I sat in the dark and drank Makers Mark and contemplated the suddenness of death. After about an hour, I called Marina and she answered immediately, obviously waiting for my call.

"Are you all right?" she asked.

"I'm fine," I said, but I'm sure she could hear the heaviness in my voice, in my soul.

"Is it over?"

"It's over," I said. "They won't be bothering you again."

"Us."

"They won't be bothering us again."

We were silent for a moment. I could hear rain beginning to patter on the roof and the patio.

"Are you coming to get me?"

"Not tonight," I said. "We've got to … decompress here."

There was a beat. "I understand."

"I'll be there first thing in the morning," I said. "I've got a meeting with Tracy."

"Yes, he told me," Marina said. "He just got back."

"I'll see you then."

We exchanged I Love Yous and then I went back to my bourbon. The rain came down heavier, until eventually it sounded like it was trying to break into the room. I could hear the hiss of tires on the parking lot outside and was envious of the tourists that were also staying here. They were out having dinner with their loved ones, enjoying fine Hawaiian cuisine, and probably drinking too many Mai Tais. They were laughing, they were delighted by cocktails with fiery garnishes. They were living life.

I was in my room with four paid killers, thinking about the five men whose lives we'd just ended, and praying that Gruber's team got things scoured before the authorities got wind that something was up.

They always did.

The bourbon did what it was supposed to do, and I suddenly couldn't keep my eyes open. I left the bottle on the nightstand and crawled into bed.

The rhythm of the rain, as loud as an earthquake, lulled me to sleep.

CHAPTER THIRTY-THREE

By the time the sun made its appearance the following morning, the rain had stopped and the clouds had dissipated enough so that it was sunnier than it was gloomy. The world smelled wet; the rain had soaked deep into the greenery surrounding us and the air had a damp, fresh smell.

I stood near the open sliding glass door of my bedroom, dressed in only a pair of boxers, and inhaled the warm, invigorating air. It was about 7am. My head felt fuzzy, and a faint headache kept tapping me annoyingly between the eyes. It was a small price to pay for the anesthetic effects I so desperately needed after last night's mission.

I slipped on a pair of cargo shorts and a *Stranger Things* t-shirt and stepped out into the living room. Jesus was sitting on the couch there, pulling on a pair of socks, and he nodded a good morning to me.

"Morning," I said. There was no point in asking if he slept well.

Puño was out on the lanai, sitting at the table with Miguel and Rigoberto. I grabbed a Coke Zero from the fridge, slid the screen door open and joined them.

"Morning," Puño said. Miguel and Rigoberto mumbled something that could have been the same thing.

"Morning," I said. I popped the top of my Coke Zero and took a big swig. It was like life was being poured back into me.

"How can you drink that shit," Puño said. "At seven o'clock in the morning?"

"I can drink this shit any hour of the day."

"Drink a Monster or something," Puño said. "Get some energy."

"Red Bull," Miguel suggested quietly.

"How about some coffee?" Rigoberto said, and I was surprised at the anger in his tone. "Doesn't anybody drink fucking coffee anymore?"

We sat quietly for a moment. "Anybody want some breakfast?" I asked. "We've got eggs and bacon in the fridge, and I think there's still some cereal left."

"What kind of cereal?" Puño asked.

"Cheerios," I said. "Maybe some Cap'n Crunch."

"The Cap'n!" Puño said excitedly. He got to his feet, maneuvered past me, and headed for the kitchen.

"Beautiful here," Miguel said, indicating the vast ocean in front of us with a sweep of his hand.

"It is," I agreed. "They say you can see whales out there sometimes …"

"No shit."

"… but so far I've seen nothing."

Rigoberto was doing something with his phone. "I'm going to do a McDonald's run," he said. "Uber's on the way. Anybody want anything?"

"Yeah, I'll take a Sausage McMuffin combo," Miguel said. "With a coffee. Black."

"Write that shit down," Rigoberto told him. "I'll forget."

"You'll forget a Sausage McMuffin combo? It ain't that hard."

"I'll forget," Rigoberto repeated. "Write it down."

He turned and hollered through the screen door. "Jesus! Want something from McDonald's?"

"Big Mac and fries!" Jesus yelled back.

"They aren't serving burgers yet, dumb ass," Rigoberto said. "It's seven in the morning!"

"Egg McMuffin then," Jesus said. "Hash Browns and coffee."

"How do you want your coffee?"

"Black, two sugars."

"Write it down."

Puño stuck his head through the doorway, a heaping bowl of Cap'n Crunch in his hand. "Someone making a Mikkey Dee's run?"

"Yeah. I am," Rigoberto said.

"Well, shit, man, nothing like waiting 'til I fill a bowl of cereal to let me know."

"I just decided," Rigoberto said. "Want something or not? Make it fast. Uber's almost here."

Puño stared down at his bowl of cereal. "Yeah, I'll take two Sausage McGriddles ..."

"Write it down," Rigoberto said. He turned to me. "Brace? You in?"

I just laughed. "No, thanks," I said. "I've got a meeting with Tracy Vang in just over an hour."

"Suit yourself," Rigoberto said. The others brought him their orders, all written on various pieces of paper, and he gathered them up and headed out the door.

Thus was breakfast with my team of assassins.

CHAPTER THIRTY-FOUR

I went downstairs at 8:30 just to take a quick walk and inhale some more of that delicious island air but I was surprised to see a Crown Vic waiting in the parking lot. A driver I didn't recognize stood at the rear door and, when he saw me, he quickly moved to open it.

"Good morning, Mr. Heller," said the driver. "Mr. Vang asked me to pick you up."

"Where's Alika?" I asked.

"Off today."

"Well, I guess everyone needs a day off," I said.

"That is true, sir."

I hopped into the back seat of the Vic and settled myself while the driver came around the front and got behind the driver's seat.

"I'm sorry," I said. "What was your name?"

"Kevin."

"Kevin. You worked for Mr. Vang long?" I asked.

"Not really," Kevin said, but didn't elaborate. "Would you like to stop anywhere on the way? Get a coffee or something?"

"Nah, I'm good," I said. "Let's just head straight there."

"Of course, sir."

I sat back, enjoying the warm envelopment of the Vic's comfortable back seat, and checked my phone. No new messages, no new e-mails (other than someone wanting to sell me the miracle of solar panels) and no voice mail. Either I was off the grid because I was out of the service area or my life had just become dull again.

I was okay with dull again.

But it wasn't to be dull for long, I realized. Even though I had eliminated the threat to my family I had done nothing to prove that Malu was innocent. All I had uncovered was a real estate deal that could easily have provided motive for murder, but it sure as hell didn't *prove* murder. So far, Malu and his buddy—the still-in-hiding Hilo—were the only suspects. I wasn't looking forward to sitting down with Tracy this morning and telling him I still had basically nothing. Yet I remained confident. I believed that Malu had not killed Matt Akana and I was convinced that I could eventually prove it. I just didn't know how long it would take and time was running out.

At this point, Hilo was the key. If I could get him to come forward, to tell his side of the story, it might be enough for the KPD to realize neither he nor Malu was the killer. But there were so many hurdles to cross there. First, there was the whole illegal alien situation. Assuming I could even convince Hilo to come forward, it would put his parents in the crossfire. A man and woman who had lived here for nearly twenty years would probably be de-ported and have their livelihoods taken from them. I wasn't happy that they were illegal, but I also didn't want to destroy a family that had been living, growing, and serving their community for nearly two decades.

Then there was the fact that Hilo was not exactly the world's greatest witness. He was well-known for his predilection for pot, he was part of a robbery gang, and his very testimony not only proved his friend's innocence, but his own as well. Would the Kauai DA buy Hilo's side of the story for even a second? Or would they write him off as a druggie who was only trying to save his own hide?

There had to be another way but, as of that moment, I had nothing.

I felt the Crown Vic slow and looked up. Kevin was pulling the car into a turn lane that was marked by a sign with an arrow pointing left and the words "Kilauea Lighthouse." My brow furrowed. The turn-off for Tracy's place was at least another ten minutes away.

"Um, are you going the right way?" I asked.

"Gotta make a quick stop," Kevin said. "Sorry."

Something wasn't right. Limo drivers didn't make "quick stops" out of the blue.

"Where are you taking me?" I asked after a moment. I tried the rear door handle. It was locked.

"Someone would like a word," Kevin said. And the professional courtesy in his voice was suddenly gone, replaced with a cold steeliness.

"Who?" I asked.

The window between the driver and the passenger compartment rolled closed with an ominous hiss.

I cursed under my breath. Jay's gun was back at the apartment. There was no reason to think I'd need it at Tracy's. And why had I been stupid enough to get into the car with a stranger? Hadn't my momma always taught me not even to talk to them? I thought about kicking out the window and taking my chances jumping out. With the speed limits so low in Kauai, how much damage could it do?

But there was also part of me that wanted to see who this "someone" was who wanted to sit down and talk with me. Assuming this wasn't a line of bullshit from Kevin and that he hadn't been paid to take me out into the jungle to put a bullet in my head, I was curious to see where this would lead. My first thought that I would soon be meeting Body Odor's boss. My second thought was that I hoped he used a better deodorant than his late employee.

The good news is that the area we were driving through wasn't jungle at all. Instead, the streets were lined with what looked like low-income houses—well, low-income for Kauai, of course. Some of them looked nice and well taken care of. Others were in various states of disrepair. We drove by one house that had apparently burned down in the past year or so and had never been re-built. Tall weeds grew up through its exposed floorboards and along charred half-walls.

Then those homes began to thin and soon we were out of that neighborhood. There was a marked improvement in the condition of the road. We came to yet another grouping of houses, perched on a cliff, with a view that, if God were a painter, he would be happy to sign his name right there in the lower corner. The houses were massive, mansions really, and huge patches of lush, green lawn stretched widely between them.

We drove up to a black iron gate and Kevin hit a button on a remote clipped to his sun visor. The gate swung open silently and the Vic pulled through.

The house behind the gate was mammoth, with a circular red brick driveway leading up to a garage door made with dark, expensive-looking wood. Kevin turned the Vic in with a smooth sweeping turn. He brought the car to a stop and got out, coming around to open the back door for me.

As I stepped out, I noticed a pathway beside the garage leading up to the main house. There stood a Hawaiian woman in a crisp grey pants suit, a clipboard or tablet of some kind clutched to her chest. She smiled as I stepped out of the Vic.

"Mr. Heller," she said. "Thank you so much for joining us."

"Thanks for the invitation," I said. "Although I would have preferred the option to R.S.V.P."

The woman laughed as though I was making a lighthearted joke at a cocktail party. "My name is Akiko," she said, extending her hand. I took it. Her grip was firm and professional, her skin the kind of soft and smooth you get from using keyboards instead of shovels as your daily work tools. "I am Mr. Papalia's assistant."

I nodded. "Pardon my French," I said. "But who the fuck is Mr. Papalia?"

Akiko laughed again. "Allow me to introduce you," she said and, taking my arm, guided me along the path to the front door.

We walked straight through the house, Akiko keeping me moving at a steady clip. I didn't get much chance to see what was inside, except that it was lush. Lots of marble, lots of expensive rugs, lots of dark wood furniture, lots of glass chandeliers. We went through a kitchen that was the size of most warehouses and through a sliding glass door to a wooden deck outside. The view of the glistening ocean from the deck would have taken my breath away if I didn't have so much else on my mind.

A man sat at a marble table on the deck, reading something from yet another tablet of some kind. Didn't anybody read newspapers anymore? There was a cup of coffee beside him and a half-eaten scone. Although he was sitting, he appeared to be a big man, well over six feet tall and probably hitting 275 pounds. His skin was a light olive color and had been browned even darker by the Kauai sun. He wore a luxurious brown robe, beneath which I could see only a plain white t-shirt that looked as though it had just come out of the package. For all I knew, he could be naked from the waist down.

I hoped not.

The man looked up when we approached and Akiko extended her hand, palm upward. "Mr. Brace Heller," she announced. The man stood and I breathed a sigh of relief to see he was indeed wearing a pair of black sweatpants. "Mr. Heller," Akiko continued. "Mr. Papalia."

"Brace, thanks for coming," Papalia said. His voice was thick and surprisingly warm and there was a trace of a Bronx accent, but only a trace. "Can I get you a coffee or something?"

"Got any Coke Zero?" I asked.

"Honey, get him a Coke, would you?" Papalia asked Akiko.

"Coke Zero," I repeated.

"All right, Coke Zero," Papalia replied, "If we got it, it's yours."

Akiko hurried off to get my beverage and Papalia indicated the chair beside him. I pulled it away from the table and took a seat. It was even heavier than I anticipated.

"Hope I didn't ruin your morning," Papalia said. "But you and me, Brace, we gotta talk."

"I'm all ears," I said.

"Brace," Papalia said, moving his mouth around the word like it was a cough drop. "What kind of name is that? I mean, I've heard Bryce and Bruce, but where the hell does Brace come from?"

"Have to ask my parents," I said. "I never really thought about it."

"Not that it's a bad name," Papalia said, patting my hand with meaty fingers. "In fact, I like it. Might even suggest one of my grandkids takes that name. Just never heard it before."

"Um. Thanks?" I said.

Papalia gave me a curious glance. "Look, I get it," he said. "You don't like being hauled away from your house first thing in the morning. I wouldn't either. You got places to go and things to do, am I right?"

I nodded. Akiko came back with my Coke Zero. She had already taken the time to open it. I could just imagine her using a fork or spoon to pry the tab up so she wouldn't break one of her precious fingernails.

"Coke Zero! I knew we had it!" Papalia said. "*Salud.*" He picked up his coffee and held it out until I clinked it with my can of soda.

"You enjoying Kauai?" Papalia asked.

"Not so far," I said. "Working."

"Oh, yeah. I get that, too. But see, here's the thing. I *want* you to enjoy Kauai. I want you to have a good time while you're here." He paused and gave me an emotionless smile. "That's all *I* ever want. I want to have a good time while I'm here." He took a sip of coffee and asked, "How often you get out here?"

"This is my first time."

"Really? That's a shame. I'm here five, six times a year. Great place, really. Paradise. Except for all the goddamn chickens, am I right?"

He tapped my hand again and laughed.

"But see, here's the problem," Papalia said. "I really haven't enjoyed my time here this visit. And you know why? Because of you, Brace. Because of you."

I raised my eyebrows innocently.

"See, you come over here, Brace, and you start sticking your nose where it don't belong," Papalia said, leaning back in his seat and giving me a hard look.

I gave it right back to him. "So, I guess those were your suits following me the other day, out to Ke'e Beach," I said.

Papalia looked surprised. "You pegged them? They didn't say anything to me about getting pegged."

"Would you expect them to?" I asked.

"No, I guess not," Papalia said. "But that's not the point. The point is that you're digging into things that aren't your business. Things that you should, plainly put, stay the fuck out of."

"I'm here as part of a murder investigation," I said. "I'm being paid to find out who killed a man. That makes everything my business."

"Not the way I see it, Brace," Papalia said. "What does your murder have to do with my deal at Hanakapi'ai Beach?"

There it was. Circle completed. "My murder victim was the real estate agent that you were working with on your Hanakapi'ai Beach Project," I said. "That's what it has to do with it."

"No, it don't," Papalia said. "That local boy killed that real estate agent. He did it for money. Money for drugs. Got nothing to do with me."

"We both know that isn't the case," I said. "And I'm not about to let that boy go to jail for the rest of his life for something he didn't do."

Papalia sat back in his chair and looked at me for a long time. He took a deep breath and another sip of coffee.

"You working for Vang?" he asked after a moment.

"That's confidential," I said.

"That's bullshit," Papalia said. "I already know you're working for Vang."

I shrugged.

Papalia suddenly grinned. "Well, that's where you fucked up, buck-o," he said. "Because you know those guys you took out last night?"

I said nothing.

"Yeah, well, it was one of them who took out that real estate agent. And now you've killed *him*. Kinda fucked up your own investigation, didn't you, shamus? Can't really ask him any questions now, can ya?"

Again, I said nothing. I could see anger starting to burn behind Papalia's eyes.

"Oh, I get that, too," Papalia said. "Marty told me he kidnapped your wife. Stupid fucker. I knew as soon as he told me that that he was gonna wind up dead. And, sure as shit, he did. At least I'm assuming he did. Haven't heard from him since yesterday afternoon and my guys tell me that the body shop is wiped clean." He grinned again. "Scrubbed, you might say."

I shrugged. "So where does that leave us?" I asked.

"That leaves you up shit creek," Papalia said. "Your murder investigation is done. Now you can get the hell off my island."

"No," I said. "I'm not leaving until the murder charge against Malu is dropped."

Papalia's face wrinkled up. "Really? *Malu*? And I thought Brace was a bad name."

His tablet dinged. He picked it up, typed in a few words, and then dropped it back on the table.

"So where does that leave us?" I asked again.

"You know, I could have a bullet put in your head right now, right here" he said. "You think your cleaners are good? Mine are better. No one would ever know you'd been here."

"Maybe. But I've been working with the KPD from Day One. Do you think they're going to assume I just tucked my tail between my legs and went home?"

"No, but I got people on the KPD."

"Not all of them."

Papalia nodded. "Yeah, probably not enough of them." He sighed. "Okay, so what will it take to get you off my island and out of my hair?"

"I want Malu cleared," I said. "When I can prove that I'm out of here."

"I can't help you with that."

"Well, then we have nothing more to discuss." I stood.

"What do you want me to do, shamus?" Papalia asked. "You want me to have one of my guys confess to the murder so your friend can get off? Ain't gonna happen."

"You'll think of something," I said.

"Say I do," Papalia said. "Say I think of something."

"Then you and I will have no further business and I can get back home."

Papalia laughed suddenly. "You want to know the funniest thing?" he said. "That goddamn beach is worthless to me. That fucking agent let me spend almost half a million dollars, promising me that everything was going to work out. Said he could grease the right palms, said he had friends in high places." He laughed again. "Turns out he couldn't and didn't. Turns out it didn't matter. I needed a port, a place to ship and receive particular ... um ... *goods*, let's say, for some pretty serious investors. And the water over there is too rough. They tell me I'd have lost more product in sinking ships than would have made it to dry land."

He shook his head, laughed again and then looked down at his hands. He was silent for a moment and then said, "I'll see what I can work out. I ain't promising anything, but I'll see what I can work out."

"Then I'll wait to hear from you," I said, turning. I stopped and turned back. "Um ... can I get a ride back to my place?"

"No," Papalia said. "Take a fuckin' Uber."

CHAPTER THIRTY-FIVE

Turns out the only Uber driver available couldn't pick me up for almost forty-five minutes so I switched tactics and called Alika. I was in his limo and on my way to Tracy's place in half the time.

"How you holding up?" I asked him. Everyone reacts differently to killing a man and, although I had no doubt that Alika had done it before, I was concerned about how last night's incident had left him.

He looked at me through the rearview mirror and his eyes were clear. "I'm fine, sir," he said. "Thank you for asking."

We drove in silence all the way to Tracy's house. I felt my pulse increase when I saw Marina standing on the front porch, her long black hair blowing in the gentle Hawaiian breeze. The anxious, concerned pinch to her face, however, left a hollow pit in my stomach.

"Where have you been?" she called in a voice that was equal parts concern and anger. "I was worried."

"I had a last-minute meeting with a new friend," I told her, trying to smile reassuringly. "Well, 'friend' may be too strong a word. Let's say business acquaintance."

She looked up at me with puzzled eyes.

"I'll tell you all about it later," I said. "I'm already late for my meeting with Tracy."

"I know," Marina said. "He and Malu are waiting out on the lanai."

I gave her a quick kiss and walked up the steps to the door, then moved through the house and past the sliding glass door to the lanai. Tracy and Malu sat there, remnants of their breakfasts scattered across china plates, a half-pitcher of orange juice between them.

"Heard you got held up a little this morning," Tracy said, standing to give me a hug.

"Yeah, got a little side-tracked," I said. "All good, though. In the long run."

"Really?"

"I think so," I said. "We'll see."

Tracy took his seat by his son. Malu looked up at me expectantly.

"So, what you got?" Tracy said with that luminescent smile of his. "Good news, I hope."

"Well, not bad news," I said. "But we've still got a ways to go."

Tracy nodded happily but Malu's shoulders slumped.

"One thing I know for certain now is that Malu didn't kill Matt Akana." I saw both Tracy and Malu sit up straighter. "Unfortunately, I can't prove that yet."

"Why not?" Malu said.

"Because, despite my sterling reputation and rugged good looks, the authorities aren't simply going to just take my word for it."

"What about Hilo?" Tracy said. "Did you track him down?"

"I did. But I don't think he's much good to us as a witness."

"Why not?" Tracy and Malu asked, virtually in tandem.

"Because he's a pothead and a felon," I said, deciding to keep his parents' illegal status to myself for now. "And he's basically testifying to save not only your skin, but his own, too."

"But you said you know we didn't do it," Malu said.

"I do," I said. "They don't."

"Do you know who did it then?" Tracy asked.

"I do," I said. "But that doesn't do us any good, either."

"Why not?"

"Because he's dead," I said. "And that leaves us hanging."

"So, what's next?" Tracy asked after a moment.

"I'll keep digging," I said. "Eventually, I'll find someone who can help us, somebody who knows something about the murder, or even saw something suspicious. Or someone who can put Malu and Hilo at another location at the time of the murder. Or I'll find some tourist photo or video. Everyone's got a smartphone these days. Or something else. But I can't give you a time frame. I'm doing the best I can."

Tracy nodded and tapped the table in front of me. "I know that, Brace," he said. "We appreciate it."

"The one thing I can't help with is the robbery charge," I said. "You're going to have to take the heat for that, Malu, and do the time." He looked at me as though he were about to argue the point, but I stopped him with the palm of my hand. "It's the right thing to do and you brought it on yourself," I said. "Your father will hire you a good lawyer and you'll take your lumps like anyone else would do. And, hopefully, you'll never do anything stupid like that again."

"He won't," Tracy said firmly.

But Malu was a kid, and I knew there were no promises in life.

"So, we're good," I said, standing. "For now."

"We're good," Tracy said, standing and shaking my hand. "Thanks, Brace."

Malu nodded but said nothing.

"Then, if you don't mind, gentlemen, I'd like to spend the day with my wife."

Tracy gave the blazing smile again. "I wouldn't have it any other way," he said.

CHAPTER THIRTY-SIX

Marina and I decided to take a visit to Waimea Canyon, which was literally on the other side of the island from The Cliffs but whose boundless, mesmerizing beauty was sung by anyone who'd ever been there. We stood on the road near the peak of the nearly 3,000-foot vista, looking out over the sparkling Pacific Ocean and the endless blue sky above it. It was like looking at a perfect postcard. It was so beautiful that it didn't seem real.

Marina took my hand. "How are you doing?" she asked.

I smiled. "I'm all good now," I said. "Now that you're here. Now that you're safe."

A moment passed.

"Were you scared?" I asked.

Marina thought for a moment. "I was scared, of course," she said. "But I knew you'd come get me."

"Or send Puño to come get you."

"Or send Puño," Marina smiled. "Still, it was not pleasant, let's put it that way. I was madder than anything else."

"Of course, you were," I said. "But it won't happen again," I said.

"Not with those guys," Marina said. "But you can't make any promises beyond that."

"No," I grimly admitted. "I can't."

We absorbed the natural beauty surrounding us in silence.

"Are you okay with that?" I said after a moment.

"I am," Marina said quickly. "Look, I know there are bad guys out there and I know that interacting with them is part of your job."

"Sad but true," I said.

"But I also know that there are bad guys out there no matter what job you do. There are bad guys I deal with every day."

"Con men who target the elderly," I said. "Pimps who beat up their hookers."

"Yeah, like that," Marina said. "And if I hide from them or fear them or keep looking over my shoulder then they control *my* life. They win."

"And you don't want them to win."

"Fucking A right," Marina said.

I smiled and looked at her. "Why, Marina Sanchez, what a filthy mouth you have."

"You have no idea," she said.

A grey fog was rolling in like a billowy Godzilla and it looked like they sky was soon going to be heavier with rain.

"How about …" I said, wiggling my eyebrows Groucho-style, "… we go back to town and try a few Mai Tais?"

"Don't they have anything else to drink on this is-land?"

"Sure," I said. "But what would be the point?"

Maria laughed. "Mai Tais it is."

And we went back to the car and set off in search of frothy libations.

CHAPTER THIRTY-SEVEN

We were at a place called Oasis on the Beach in Kapa'a, an open-air bar and grill with a thatched roof and another view to kill for. The fog had crawled away a little and the sun was fighting to get through. There was a cool gentle breeze that never got too cold.

I was drinking a Mai Tai and Marina had a martini made with pineapple-infused vodka and blackberry drizzle. Marina's was prettier but mine was tastier. In fact, it was the best Mai Tai I'd had in Kauai so far.

We were chatting with a bartender named Zeke, a friendly young man boasting slick tribal tattoos twisted tightly around his daily work-out biceps. Zeke was telling us the secret of the Oasis Mai Tai which was the orgeat syrup they made fresh every morning. I had no idea what orgeat was and was about to inquire when my phone rang. It was Jay Huihui.

"Have you ever had the Mai Tais at Oasis at the Beach?" I said, answering the phone. "I think they're the best on Kauai."

"Don't drink Mai Tais," Jay said. "That's a tourist cocktail."

"Maybe you've just never had one with orgeat, whatever the hell that is," I told him. "What's up?"

"I thought you'd want to know," Jay said. "They just dropped the charges against your boy."

"Wait. What? Who did?"

"The D.A.," Jay continued. "Apparently, a new witness came forward, says they saw somebody go into that bathroom just after your boys came out."

"Who'd they see?"

"Six feet two inches or so of bald black man," Jay said. "Big cinder block in his hands."

"Ring any bells?"

"I personally don't know any six foot two bald black men."

"I know one," I said. "But he lives in Boston. And he's fictional."

"Somehow I doubt it's him."

"Probably not," I said. "Who's the witness?"

"Dentist over in Lihue," Jay said.

A dentist is a better witness than a distracted volleyball player or a high-as-a-kite pothead, I thought.

"You told the Vangs?"

"Not yet," Jay said. "You did the work. Thought I'd tell you first. Gonna call them next."

"I didn't do anything," I said.

"Bullshit," Jay said. "If nothing else, you stirred the pot. Got things going."

"Maybe."

"So, I take it this means you'll be going back to the Mainland?" Jay asked.

"I guess so."

"Wanna catch a drink before you head back?"

"I'd like that," I said. "But I don't think there will be time."

"Heading back so soon?"

"Gotta get the wife back to work."

Marina smiled, sipped at her martini.

"Thanks, Jay," I continued. "I appreciate all your help, man. I'll leave your piece with Alika. Will that work?"

"Yeah, that's fine," Jay said. "I'll get it from him later. Hey, Brace."

"Yeah?"

"Orgeat is a kind of almond liqueur."

I snapped my fingers. "That makes perfect sense."

We disconnected the call.

"Did I hear that right?" Marina asked.

"You did," I told her. "Orgeat is a type of almond liqueur."

Marina punched my arm. "Not that, you twit. Did he say they dropped the charges against Malu?"

"That's what he said."

"How did that happen?"

I looked at her and shrugged. "Probably something to do with a mob guy with well-cared for teeth," I said. "But how the hell do I know?"

I went back to my Mai Tai while Marina gazed at me with a puzzled and annoyed look.

CHAPTER THIRTY-EIGHT

My office hadn't changed much in the ten days I'd been gone.

The anteroom was still cold and empty, except for the loose stack of unread mail which was splayed across the floor. Most of it was useless but some of it was fast food coupons and, in the life of a private eye, those usually came in handy.

The main office was just as cold and just as empty. The phone sat silently on the desk, belligerently refusing to ring. The computer monitor gave me a blank stare as I came around the desk. A red dot flashed in its lower right-hand corner. Apparently, I had turned off the PC before I left but neglected to do the same for the monitor. The only sound was the humming of the compact refrigerator in the corner and the soft mumble of traffic passing on the street below.

I peeled off my Motorhead baseball cap, tossed it at the hat rack near the fridge, and hooked it on the first try. Two points! The chair behind my desk sighed with discomfort as I collapsed into it. One of these days, I'd have to replace it. It wasn't that I didn't have the money for it (thanks to Tracy, I did), but I was too lazy to go shopping and then lug a new chair up to the second story.

I glanced at the answering machine and saw no flashing red light there. No messages. With nothing else to do, I began sorting through the tangled mess of mail.

Apparently, I had missed a couple of sales at Target while I was gone, Solar Panels were THE BRIGHT ALTERNATIVE, and I could buy one Bacon Ultimate Cheeseburger and get one free at Jack in the Box. I dumped it all into the trash, except for the Jack coupons, of course, which I neatly tucked into the desk drawer so I could instantly forget they were there until they were well expired.

Back at work. Back at home. Now what?

The phone rang, its shrill *bbrrringg* shattering the morning peace. It made me flinch and, for a moment, I thought about shooting it. My calmer side prevailed, however, and I picked up the receiver.

"Heller Investigations," I said into the mouthpiece.

"Brace! It's Tracy!"

"Long time no see, brah," I said.

"Yeah, it's been like thirty-six hours. Hey! I just wanted to thank you again for all you did here. I knew I could count on you."

"I did what I could," I said. "And thanks for fifty Gs. Between you and DiabetiCorp, I'm set for a while."

"You earned it," Tracy said. "And who the heck is DiabetiCorp?"

"Not important," I told him. "How's Malu doing?"

"So far, so good," Tracy said. "He's got a court date for the robbery thing, and I've hired him a really good lawyer."

"He needs to know what he did was wrong, Tracy. He needs to know there's a price to pay. You can't have a lawyer just make this go away."

"I know," Tracy said after a moment, and I could hear the change in his tone. "I'm just trying to minimize the damage."

"I understand," I said. "You're a good dad."

We were both silent for a moment and then Tracy's chipper attitude returned. "So, anyway, I just wanted to say thanks again and to tell you that you and Marina are always welcome here. You've got a place to stay."

"And a driver?" I laughed.

Tracy laughed, too. "I don't think Alika would have it any other way. I think he kinda loves you, man."

"Yeah, well, I kinda love him, too," I said. "Thanks for calling, Tracy. Hopefully, we'll see each other soon ... and under better circumstances."

"That would be all right with me," Tracy said. "Bye, Brace."

"Bye." I dropped the receiver back into the cradle.

For the next couple of hours, I went through the newspapers, circling some articles that interested me. There weren't many. I turned on the computer and did some much-needed research. Apparently, the Foo Fighters had released a new video and I figured that, as a trained detective, I should watch it on YouTube in case I needed to refer to it later as evidence. I paid a few bills. Hell, I paid all the bills. My bank account was now as fat as Baron Harkonnen from *Dune*.

Just before noon, I saw the shadow of the outside door open and, a split second later, Puño entered the room.

"What up?" he said.

"Spoke to Tracy this morning," I told him. "Malu's court date is set."

"Stupid little shit."

"True that," I said. "Hopefully, he'll get his head screwed on right."

"Hope in one hand and shit in the other," Puño said.

"And see which one fills up first. I know."

We sat there for a while, enjoying the relative silence, both of us considering something that the other was unaware of.

"You want tacos?" Puño said after a while.

"Hell to the yeah," I said. "Where do you want to go?"

"That Mondo's place still around?"

"Nah, man. Closed."

"Damn. Them were some good tacos."

"They were."

"Amigos?"

"Closed now, too," I said. "Apparently, tacos are not well respected in Downtown Ventura."

"*Pinche gringos*," Puño growled. "Where then?"

"Limon Y Sal," I said. "I don't know about the tacos, but they make a mean margarita. Big one, too."

"Who needs tacos?" Puño said brightly.

"Not me."

And out we went.

Chapter Thirty-Nine

I was with Marina, leaning against the wooden rails near the end of the Ventura Pier. The weather was cool but brought with it the warm promise of the coming summer. Gulls circled above us, crying about their day to whoever would listen. Occasionally, a lone feather would slowly see-saw to the wooden planks or slip through the cracks to continue their journey to the sea below. It was quiet except for the cool hiss of the breeze, the quiet mumbling of the nearby fisherman and the seawater lapping against barnacle-encrusted pylons.

I was in my standard uniform—shorts, t-shirt, and sandals—wishing I'd brought along a sweatshirt or windbreaker to take the edge off, while Marina stood next to me in a flowered sundress, basking in both the golden sun and the bracing breeze. Both of us were full of lunch and cocktails—fried shrimp and French fries for me, a hamburger (no onions) for Marina and a Cadillac margarita for each of us.

It was late afternoon, and the air was so clear it seemed you could reach out and touch the Channel Islands.

Life was good.

"You know," I said. "I really see no reason to go back to Hawaii."

Marina gave me a look. "Why do you say that?"

"Look at this," I said, sweeping my arm toward the horizon. "We've got all the sun we can use, the sky is as blue as a baby blanket, and we're ten minutes from home. What has Hawaii got that California doesn't?"

Marina was quiet a moment. I could sense her considering. "You're not wrong," she said at last. "But there's just something about it, isn't there? I mean, we were only there a few days, and not under the best of circumstances, but I can't wait to go back again."

"There's a reason they call it Paradise," I said. "And we can go back whenever we want. Tracy said we can stay at his place."

Marina smiled and the world seemed to dim in deference to her brightness. She turned her back to me and fell against my chest. Spoons on the pier. I put my arms around her and held tight.

"I've got vacation time coming in October," she said. "Is that a good month to go to Hawaii?"

"Could be," I said. "I can't imagine a bad time."

"Me, either." She turned to face me, giving me a quick kiss on the lips. "But Brace …" she said.

"Yes?"

"Can we go without Puño this time?" she asked. "He's kind of a third wheel."

We laughed and kissed and took no notice of the fisherman who glared at the crazy couple who were scaring off their fish.

ABOUT THE AUTHOR

R. Scott Bolton lives in Ventura with his wife Shelley, his son Josh and his dogs, Leo, Zoey, and Pretzel. He hosts several podcasts for fun, with topics such as show-biz and liquor, and you can listen to them by visiting his podcast studio at www.RoughEdgeFM.com.

Scott loves to hear from readers and welcomes e-mail at rsb@rscottbolton.com.